CHARLES DEMERS
PROPERTY VALUES

ARSENAL PULP PRESS
VANCOUVER

PROPERTY VALUES

ARSENAL PULP PRESS
Suite 202 – 211 East Georgia St.
Vancouver, BC V6A 1Z6
Canada
arsenalpulp.com

The publisher gratefully acknowledges the support of the Canada Council for the Arts and the British Columbia Arts Council for its publishing program, and the Government of Canada, and the Government of British Columbia (through the Book Publishing Tax Credit Program), for its publishing activities.

Cover and text design by Oliver McPartlin
Edited by Susan Safyan
Printed and bound in Canada

Library and Archives Canada Cataloguing in Publication:
Demers, Charles, 1980-, author

    Property values / Charles Demers.

Issued in print and electronic formats.

ISBN 978-1-55152-727-7 (softcover).—ISBN 978-1-55152-728-4 (HTML)

    I. Title.

PS8607.E533P76 2018   C813'.6   C2017-907220-X

                                  C2017-907221-8

for my uncle Phil

"But the real obsession of the drug-traffickers, their Freudian obsession, has been to buy land, land, ever more land [...] It is as though they are trying to buy up the entire map, with its condors and its rivers, the yellow of its gold and the blue of its seas, so that no one can ever move them from where they want to be." —Gabriel García Márquez

"Homer, affordable tract housing made us neighbours, but you made us friends." —Ned Flanders

PROLOGUE: INTERIOR LIFE

"Jesus, that's good. I think that's real buckwheat. Fuck, that's nice."

"I told you, bro."

"Told me what? You never said anything about the soba. You told me to get the udon."

"I mean Kamloops, man, that it's changing. That redneck shit, that's yesterday's news."

"You don't know anything, do you?"

"What?"

"A Japanese restaurant, in the Interior—that's not from good, man."

"What are you talking about?"

"If you're in small-town BC, and you have whatever—Thai food or Indian or Jamaican or whatever—"

"I took you to that Jamaican place right here! Just up the parking lot. With that pirate on the wall."

"What pirate?"

"The black guy, the sea captain."

"That was Marcus Garvey, you dumbshit."

"I don't know who that is."

"Amazingly, I believe you."

"What, who is he?"

"Anyway, any other kind of restaurant like that, non-white, in a small town in BC, that's fine, that's from progress."

"But not Japanese?"

"Not Japanese."

"How come?"

"Because if there's good Japanese food in a town like this, it's because your grandpa took their fucking fishing boat in World War II."

"I don't get it. My grandpas were in Manitoba. I don't think they ever even seen the ocean."

"Internment, man. You meet Japanese people in one of these buttfuck places, it's because they got kicked out of Vancouver and taken here."

"Ah, I don't believe that."

"Believe? Fine, whatever. Believe what you want, dude. I'm not asking for your opinion, I'm telling you what it is. The pirate on the wall, Jesus."

"How would you even know they were from Vancouver?"

"Aside from why would they ever move here? See the pennant over by the till? The baseball pennant?"

"Asahi? That's a beer, no?"

"Asahi was the Japanese baseball team from Vancouver. Downtown Eastside. Million years ago."

"But—the chick at the register, she had an accent."

"I'm not saying they all came from the city. I'm saying somebody from this restaurant, somebody who remembered how to make these good-ass noodles and good-ass soups from Japan, they were probably in Vancouver first, and somebody made them leave."

"Jesus."

"So, you've got that in common."

"Fuck off, man, that's not funny."

"I don't know how you can do this, man. This slow, podunk redneck shit."

"Three bedrooms for three-fifty, bro. That's all you gotta know."

"So what? I can get you fifteen bedrooms in Latvia for eighty bucks Canadian. What did Danny say?"

"Danny's not my mother, man."

"No."

"Besides, Danny needs me, or Nicky needs me, or whatever, I'm three-and-a-half hours away. For some stuff, maybe it's even better I don't live in the city."

"Jesus, man. The world is changing."

The two men finished their noodles, paid the young woman with the accent at the cash register, and walked out to see the full brightness of the afternoon poured over shining vehicles that filled the strip-mall parking lot, each one looking like they'd just been washed.

"I'll give you this at least, man. It's sunnier here than in Vancouver."

"So what? Everywhere is sunnier'n Vancouver."

The clap of gunfire sounded at what seemed like the same instant the shorter man's chest crumpled.

"Brody?"

"It don't look so big from here!" yelled the shooter, squeezing three bullets into the face and stomach of the man still standing.

Kamloops shoppers from various conveniently clustered retail outlets began to scream as they processed the incongruously metropolitan violence. The tires of the red Dodge Ram screamed with them as the vehicle surged through the parking lot, turning onto one of the several smaller streets that radiated out from the shops and onto the wide, long highway that led from the rest of the whole country right into its terminus city.

1

When the murders were reported the next day, the papers were sure to note that the victims were "known to police," so that normal people wouldn't be too worried or care too much. To be known in this way implied an intimacy greater than the biblical sense of the word; for Brody Miller and Wayson Tam, the two Da Silva Brothers associates gunned down outside the Ramen Lion in Kamloops in the harsh dry sunshine of a summer afternoon, to be known to police was to be hived off from the rest of humanity, to be marked as the kind of easy-money scumbags who refused to work for a living like the rest of us. Anybody who expected an immediate seventy- or eighty-percent return on any investment, besides a house, probably deserved whatever they had coming.

The criminal enterprises of the Da Silva Brothers had deeply divided Vancouver's racist community: those who primarily saw news about them on television considered them to be emblematic of the Punjabi gangs threatening the safety of Lower Mainland taxpayers, while those who primarily heard about them on the radio considered them to represent the nightmare of Latino criminal predation. That they were neither Punjabi nor Latino perhaps got at the underlying set of circumstances that had allowed the two siblings to navigate the Vancouver underworld with such success. Born in Canada to Catholic parents from Goa, the Da Silva boys had found themselves uniquely equipped for life and death in the mosaic of organized crime on the West Coast. Vincenzo "Zio" De Angelis had been present at the first communion of Danny Da Silva's daughter, Epiphany; Nicky Da Silva had been photographed on all three days of Manpreet "Goodnite" Singh's wedding. Almost preternaturally, the Da Silva boys had developed a talent for talking with the very select groups of people whom they could not terrify or, eventually, extinguish. Like early Cold War Americans, they combined hard and soft power expertly, viewing big guns and diplomacy not as mutually exclusive alternatives but as handmaidens; like early Cold War

Americans, they prioritized talent above tribal loyalties, recruiting brains and muscle in all hues. There would be some newspaper readers who, in taking in the news of Miller and Tam's shooting, wouldn't be able to help but be oddly moved that a boy christened Brody Terrence and a boy christened Wayson Ji Yu could be members of the same gang, gunned down by the same people. It marked a certain kind of progress.

But closer observers of the city's gangland conflagrations would know that any biting at the fringes of the Da Silva organization meant that the careful equilibrium that had held the peace for several years now was starting to unravel. It had been a long time since the Da Silvas had had to prove anything, or since anyone had tried to prove anything by them. The uneasy detente between their lively multicultural ranks and those of their more homogeneously pallid, leather-vested rivals, the Underground Riders, had been hard-won, but for it to be lost didn't require malice or stupidity on anyone's part. That there were now armed men stationed inside and outside the Da Silva home in the deep suburbs of Surrey—that Epiphany and her siblings, her cousins, her mother, and her aunt had been evacuated to a suite in a soaring hotel better suited to a raucous bachelor party—didn't have to be anybody's fault; though, of course, it always could be. Peace could come apart through stupidity or entropy: a handful of arrests, retirements, malignant blood cells, or new babies; the wrong collision of personalities or resentments or misunderstandings—any of it could upset the delicate chemical balance that had, until the deaths of Brody Miller and Wayson Tam, two men known to police, kept the physics from flying through the air.

From the elliptical trainer, you could see through the half-windows above ground and onto the property that belonged to the biker. The biker was gone now, and long-dried button-down shirts on wire hangers were draped from the exercise machine.

The biker had been a charismatic curiosity for neighbours looped around the whole of Driftwood Crescent, and neither Scott nor Michelle had been exceptions. There was the baldness, neither clearly voluntary nor clearly involuntary, when usually that was so obvious; and there were tattoos somehow both inscrutable and uninteresting, like a graduate thesis, stamped across a knot of arm, neck, and back muscles the width of a ping-pong table. Whenever he was outside, in view of the neighbours, the biker seemed to keep all of his muscles in motion, stretching and rotating and loosening and tightening his body with a lack of stillness that would only have looked like weakness in a much smaller man. The impossible swollen strength of him had been a running joke between Scott and Michelle—that Michelle might actually find it very sexy, that she wanted to be held by him, to hold on to him from behind as he rode off on the giant, black and silver roar of bike that he usually kept underneath a thick cover in the garage, leaving his Escalade on the street, its windows darkened.

Scott had assumed, of course, that they were jokes—it had never occurred to him to ask. Now he'd never know.

One night, in the middle of a home-renovation show, the growl of several other bikes arriving in their neighbour's driveway had drawn their attention through the blinds behind the couch. It had been a T-shirt ride, a summer evening excursion unencumbered by safety considerations, and Scott could read the back of one of the shirts as the half-dozen loud, large men had entered through the side gate of their neighbour's yard: "If You Can Read This, The Bitch Fell Off." Scott did something acid and unpleasant with his throat, half scoffing and half tsking.

"Nice," he said impotently. "Jesus, that's gross."

Michelle had smirked. "I want a shirt that says on the front, 'If You Can Read This—Who's Driving The Bike?!'"

Scott took the shirts off the exercise machine, bunching them in his hand. He would have to start using the elliptical again, regularly. His stomach and chest, chin, and cheeks had once again become insulated with a layer of soft—an insulation from which he had thought that he himself had been insulated by a wedding band, by inertia. But just over a year ago, without even any great acrimony, Michelle had taken her jokes and her lips and was gone. And then, just a few months later, the biker too left the cul-de-sac, never putting the house up for sale but disappearing with his bike and Escalade, replaced by the kind of young family Scott had told Michelle he wasn't ready for. Now all he had was her father as a sort of business partner, and that would also have to end soon, whether he could afford it or not. They had an agreement.

Driftwood Crescent was the only place Scott had ever lived, and the prospect of having to leave terrified him. The term "nestled" is applied loosely in the vocabulary of real estate sales, but Driftwood Crescent really was, halfway down a steep hillside in the suburb of Coquitlam. Coquitlam was where the Vancouver suburbs began in earnest; Burnaby, the first municipality east of the medium-big city, huddled close to Vancouver like someone trying to get a better view at a show. But no part of Coquitlam touched Vancouver proper; the weather was different there, snowy during the coastal winter rains; garbage couldn't be put to the curb too early lest it attract bears. As soon as they could drive, teenagers in Burnaby spent their evenings and weekends in downtown Vancouver, but by the time you got to Coquitlam, the kids were just as likely to break further east, learning to drink in bars playing country music.

Scott and his friends had been among those breaking west, uninterested in the hick, big-wheel kitsch of the deep suburbs. Throughout high school, Scott had been part of a superlatively multi-ethnic crew, anathema to the prevailing vibe next to the mechanical bulls. Josiah Kim was himself the product of a mixed marriage, a Korean father and Chinese mother, meaning that whenever people guessed at Josiah's ethnicity—as they invariably did—they were always a little right and always a little wrong. Josiah's father, Ha-Chang, had taken the boys hunting as a graduation present; he had learned himself from Josiah's grandfather, who had kept his young children alive with game during a long trek from North to South toward the end of the war. Pardeep Dhaliwal's family had been in British Columbia longer than anyone else's, including Scott's, and so whenever Pardeep was asked where he was from, he would name someplace extravagantly and obscurely European, claiming alternately Estonian or Basque origins just to confound the inquisitor. Contributing to the confusion was the fact that Pardeep's parents, Gurdeep and Manjot, ran a popular Greek restaurant called Polis. Adnan abd-Husseini had been born in Cairo, then lived in Waterloo, Ontario, through the final years of elementary school before his father's interests in a men's fashion franchise brought the family west. Though Adnan moved to England for university and stayed, gradually leaving his suburban pals entirely behind—even disappearing offline in an idiosyncratic rejection of social media—his presence was immortalized by the nickname he had given the crew: the Non-Aligned Movement, named for the project helmed by Colonel Nasser, Jawarharlal Nehru, Kwame Nkrumah, and Marshal Tito, to keep the majority of the world's peoples out of obeisance to either the American or Soviet empires during the twentieth century. Adnan had explained that the Non-Aligned Movement was particularly appropriate since the white people involved were Yugoslavs, and though the name "Scott Clark" slotted the wearer into an invisible Scottishness that practically counted as ethnic wallpaper in British Columbia, it belied the Serbian contributions of his very beautiful and winningly sarcastic Balkan mother, Bojana.

The four boys, graduating high school with seventy-five-percent statistical virginity, had each saluted the Non-Aligned Movement in their yearbook quotes, though they had argued over whether it was cooler to use the initials themselves or the numerical placements of the letters, in the style of prison gangs and Kabbalists. In the end, they were split down the middle: "14-1-13 4 life," (Josiah); "14/1/13 Zindabad!" (Pardeep); "NAM forever baby" (Adnan); "NAM till I Die" (Scott). And on the sidewalk right in front of the house on Driftwood Crescent—a house that Scott was barely clinging on to through a business partnership with a man who was no longer his father-in-law—the letters N-A-M had been carved forever into concrete that had once been wet.

Scott hung the shirts in the closet where his own father's clothes had formerly hung, even though Scott still preferred to sleep in what had always been his own room.

2

"Moussaka."

"Thanks, Par, that's beautiful. You gonna sit down?"

"Eggplant and potatoes. If the *goray* in this town had had any palates when we started back in the eighties, this could have been *aloo* and *bhartha*."

"Grab a seat, man," said Scott.

"Korean restaurants did okay," Josiah put in.

"That's different," said Pardeep.

"Seriously, are you just going to stand there? It's unsettling."

"How is it different?"

"'Cause there's Koreans in Coquitlam, bro! You think *apnay* are going to drive over the bridge to get something they can already get in Surrey? We needed white people to eat it, and we knew they wouldn't. Then, I mean. Now it's all fuckin' butter chicken burritos and shit."

"Why didn't you try to get Korean customers then?"

"You're joking, right? You guys are more racist than them!"

"That's true."

"I'm just going to start eating with you looming."

"Do your thing, Scotty."

"Chinese restaurants seem to thrive in more or less any environment."

"Hey, how come Chinese or Koreans don't eat Indian food?"

"I don't know. I guess we don't need it."

"God, that's fucking delicious. Your mom's a genius, Par. You know, I think I like moussaka better than lasagne."

"What?"

"What do you mean, 'what'?"

"I don't understand the connection."

"I don't know, I mean—they're both square? Stacked, I guess?"

"Yeah, that's true—they are both layered."

"Starch, nightshade, protein."

"Tomato's not a nightshade."

"I think it is."

"No."

"He's right, it is."

Pardeep, Josiah, and Scott were each removing their phones from their pockets to research the taxonomy of tomatoes when Gurdeep Dhaliwal entered the front door carrying close to twenty litres of canola oil between two hands.

"Hey, goddamn it," he yelled, "this is a business, not *Star Trek*. Get off the goddamn communicators and take these back to the kitchen."

"Jesus, Dad, don't come in like that through the front door with the oil! Customers don't need to see that—that's why we got a kitchen door."

"You're so worried about customers, tend to them instead of these free-loaders."

"Hello, Mr Dhaliwal."

"Hi, Mr Dhaliwal."

"Josiah, Scotty. Scott, you going to pay for that meal this time?"

"Yeah, Mr Dhaliwal, of course. And for last time's too, I just forgot to hit the cash machine first."

"Dad, I keep telling you—we need to take cards!"

"Honestly, Mr Dhaliwal, he's right—nobody uses cash anymore."

"Scotty, do I come to your house and tell you who you should let rifle around in your goddamn pockets?"

"No."

"So then do me the same goddamn courtesy, hey? Visa, Mastercard—Josiah, I'm assuming you've heard the saying 'thieves in the night'?"

"Yes."

"That's because they don't want to compete with Visa during the day. Thieves in the morning, the afternoon, thieves in the night—they don't sleep. They're goddamn tapeworms, wrapped around the neck of the small businessman."

"Tapeworms don't—"

"I didn't get into business feeding white people in order to make Mastercard richer. I did it to leave an inheritance to my useless son."

"Just give me the fucking oil."

"Watch your fucking mouth, *kutha chodu!*"

"I'll pay up tonight, Mr Dhaliwal."

"Ah, your money's no good here, you dumb *gora.*"

As two generations of bickering Dhaliwals made their way into the kitchen, each carrying close to ten litres of canola oil, Scott continued to eat his moussaka and Josiah leafed through a tzatziki-splattered newspaper.

"I'm picking up *Counterinsurgency 4* tomorrow morning—you want to come by in the afternoon?" he asked, eyes still on the paper. Scott and Josiah had been playing video games against each other in the same basement, on the same street in Coquitlam, since not long after the fall of the Berlin Wall. Through late childhood and puberty, from 8-bit through to 16-bit right up to a degree of graphic immersion that gave some players motion sickness, from the hope and optimism of the end of Communism through to the more resigned realism of actual global liberty, the two had sat jostling almost motionlessly beside each other and in opposition to each other, faces impassive, thumbs a blur.

"You don't need to do any prep or anything?"

"Prep for what?"

"I don't know, September?"

"The prof I'm assisting for is in Prague until Labour Day. But it's a Thursday evening class, so he figures we can meet after he gets back."

"Prague, nice."

"Yeah."

"That'll be you some day."

"How do you figure?"

"Dr Kim."

"Yeah, man, geography is booming. Are you fucking drunk or something?"

"Anyway, I can't play *Counterinsurgency*, I got Michelle's dad. Supposed to meet him about the house."

"Any developments?"

Scott swallowed his moussaka.

"Just that I'm even further away from being able to buy him out than I was six months ago. That I can't keep up." In the Chinese style, Josiah filled Scott's water glass for him—though water, especially iced, already marked the meal as well outside of the Chinese style—and Scott responded with the almost imperceptible gratitude of a finger tapping the table, also a Chinese custom. The first time Bojana had seen him doing it, tapping the table like a blackjack player, she couldn't believe how rude her son was being until Josiah, then maybe fifteen years old, had explained to her that it was politeness, a bow in miniature, and she had laughed for a minute and a half before giving Josiah a long kiss on the forehead, flushing his narrow cheeks before she left the kitchen. When Scott had poked his head into his parents' room a few minutes later to ask if he could move his father's work stuff off the ping-pong table downstairs, he could see that Bojana had been crying. All through Scott's bucolic multicultural adolescence, Bojana would watch as her once-beloved Yugoslavia was reduced nightly to a lie on the news; she remembered the Serbs and Croats and Montenegrins and Muslim Bosnians she had grown up with, and every time her son's far-flung schoolmates gave some exotic-to-her reminder of their Canadian admixture, she tended to get sentimental.

"The house is worth probably a hundred-twenty grand more than it was a year ago. One year, Joe. That's another sixty fucking grand I owe him. I'll never be able to buy out his half if it keeps growing like that. It's like owing money to the mob."

"So then what happens?"

"We have to sell the place and each walk away with our half."

Josiah swallowed softly, staring down at the newspaper, preparing for an uncharacteristic delicacy.

"Would that be so bad?"

"It's—" Scott managed, before trailing off, scooping a few forkfuls of eggplant and trying to force it past the growing lump in his throat. Holding a vinegar-soaked towel, Pardeep approached the table again, trying to make sense of the uncanny silence between his ball-busting friends.

"What's up?"

"Scott was just—"

"I mean, that's all that's left, you know? Not just all the memories in the house, my whole life there. If I sell that house, that's it. I have nothing left of her."

"Who are we talking about? Michelle?"

Scott took a sip from his water.

"No."

"Here's what I don't understand," offered Josiah. "You say the house is worth a hundred and twenty thousand more than it was a year ago. And you say it like it's a bad thing."

"Fuck," said Pardeep. "I remember when my dad used to brag to his cousin in Saskatoon that our house was *worth* a hundred and ninety."

"That's still pretty impressive for Saskatoon."

"Par, let him finish," Scott said, leaning forward.

"If Michelle's dad were invested in any other stock that had gone up twelve percent last year, was guaranteed to go up that or more next year, and the year after that—would he cash out?"

"I don't know. I guess not?"

"Why would he? Guy bet the right number on a broken roulette wheel."

"Well—they wouldn't keep spinning it."

"Huh?"

"I don't understand," said Pardeep. "In this scenario, the casino guy, he just keeps spinning? He doesn't fix it?"

"I don't think I can work with this kind of stupidity."

Pardeep snapped the vinegar-wet towel against the side of Josiah's neck. "*Bhenchode!*"

"Ow! Goddamn it, that hurt."

"Would you two shut the fuck up? Joe, what are you saying?"

"He's saying Michelle's dad has no reason to want to cash out. Fuck, man, that's probably what he wants to see you for."

"You think?"

"Why would he? You said yourself, it's like he's the mob. The vigorish is going to keep growing—if he's sixty grand richer after just a year, in five it'll be more than a quarter million."

"That's actually true," Scott said, a wave of relief pushing several bits of moussaka to his mouth in quick succession.

"What the goddamn hell is wrong with you!" It wasn't spoken as a question, but as a declaration from the door to the kitchen, directed at his son. "I sent you to get Josiah, not to convene a bloody meeting of the United Nations. *Chulloh!*"

"Oh, right—Joe, my dad wants you back there."

"What? Why?"

"The electrician is here, Tanaka. He thinks if you're back there, Tanaka will give him a discount."

"Well, congratulations—that's maybe the most offensive thing I've heard all year."

"Yeah."

"Your dad doesn't know much about Japanese-Chinese-Korean relations, huh?"

"You can tell him yourself. But as long as somebody's referring to him as an Arab on at least a weekly basis, I doubt he's going to feel too bad."

The boys stood from the table, heading back to the kitchen, Pardeep playfully slapping Josiah's newspaper against Scott's chest as they left. Flush with cautious optimism, Scott was already giddy, bouncing his knee rapidly and picking at the Greek salad on the fringes of his plate when he looked down and saw the pencil drawing of Angelique Bryan, the *Vancouver Star*'s stalwart crime reporter and biweekly law-and-order columnist. There was something about Bryan's Caribbean features that made even the shoulders-up drawing which accompanied her pieces impossibly sexy to Scott, and he would often read her columns even though he hated her politics. It wasn't that she was openly conservative, a political philosophy forbidden to him not so much through his own line of inquiry as from an osmosis inheritance of values from his mother, who never stopped bragging about the Partisans in her family tree who had jumped down from the thick branches to slit Nazi throats. Bryan didn't demonstrate any of the free-marketeering or immigrant-blaming hallmarks of bellicose right-wingers; she just seemed to share their zeal for locking up bad guys and losing the keys. She was smarter than the shock jocks, too, building elegant sentences and elegant arguments, augmented in their persuasiveness, for Scott, by the face next to the byline. Already half smiling, and a quarter excited, he began reading.

WELL, THERE STAYS THE NEIGHBOURHOOD

Angelique Bryan

Okay—that's one way to do it.

For what feels like eternity, the supposed greatest policy minds in the world have been helpless before the Sphinx's riddle of Metro Vancouver's overheated housing market. But the residents of Raven Place, a quiet Surrey street like almost any other (except for a few infamous neighbours) have learned that it may take a hail of bullets to stop Lower Mainland real estate from moving.

The brazen daylight murders of alleged Da Silva Brothers soldiers Brody Miller and Wayson Tam sent shockwaves through local law enforcement circles. It appeared to many worried observers in blue that the uneasy alliance struck four years ago between the alleged crime family and their outlaw biker rivals, the Underworld Riders, might be coming to an end. That's no surprise—we'd expect law enforcement to be wary. But realtors?

"I've really never seen anything like it," offered one local real estate agent who—a first in the history of realtors—asked to remain anonymous. "We've got multiple units along Raven Place that should be moving incredibly quickly. Amazing redevelopment and rezoning opportunities, as well as some units that are perfect as is. But we can't even get viewers, let alone offers."

Imagine that—a house in Greater Vancouver worth leaving standing after you buy it! How is it possible that a gem so rare could be stuck on the market?

Well, would you like to meet your new neighbours?

It would appear that the black hole of Raven Place real estate prices is a wide, pink, two-storey home that isn't even for sale. The home is registered to a Magdu Da Silva, 67. But anyone on Raven Place will tell you who else lives there: her notorious nephews, Danny and Nicky.

With reports that the Da Silvas are taking major security precautions, stationing cars full of large men outside a property already patrolled by a family of pearl-grey pit bulls, it would appear that prospective buyers have cooled to the once peaceful area.

"It never used to be a problem," one neighbour tells me, also asking not to be named or described. "You almost never see them, and the aunt seems very sweet. Guys come and go from the house, but there were never any big parties or nothing. One winter, these big guys shovelled out everybody's driveways on the block. To be honest, in a way we felt safer having them there."

But the appeal of that, shall we say, unorthodox, Neighbourhood Watch has clearly waned.

"I know one family, the dad got a job in Calgary, but they haven't been able to sell the house. Nothing's moving for blocks. Nobody wants to be caught in the crosswires."

I'm pretty sure my source meant 'crossfire'—but it's fair to say that on Raven Place, the wires are crossed. A community that once found security, maybe even a vicarious thrill, from its proximity to local gangster royalty is finding the crown weighs pretty heavy these days.

abryannewsblotter@vanstar.com

Scott rolled his eyes, pounding back the rest of the water that Josiah had poured for him, smiling. At least now he had a Plan B.

3

Scott entertained deep thoughts about the masculinity of his drink as he waited at the counter for a decaffeinated London Fog. Directly behind him in line had been a looming young man, gargle breathing, and Scott could see now that he was very tall, and was as fat as he was muscular, which was a lot in either direction. The man wore two large diamond studs in each ear and a small purse that looked like nothing so much as underwear as it stretched to breaking underneath a mound that was half breast and half pectoral. The earrings and the purse should theoretically have been more feminine than Scott's frothed milk and bergamot, but on the man, with his surfeit of masculinity, the womanly accents seemed almost satirical: this was a scrotum with pigtails. A post–9/11 era chin-strap beard went its way from his ears along his jaw, barely hours ahead of the stubble that rushed to catch up with it. Once he had his black coffee, the man poured half of it into a garbage can despite an advisory sign prohibiting same, filled the cup with milk and then multiple packets of sugar, which was childish, but nobody was liable to call him out on it because his T-shirt—which was working desperate overtime—read "You Are Here."

The You Are Here T-shirts had become the sine qua non of suburban sartorial machismo over the past several years. The copyright for the slogan was held by the legal, corporate office of the Underground Riders Motorcycle Club, and while a full-patch member wouldn't need to sport it, the line of T-shirts, hats, and stickers were an easy way for aspiring associates to declare theoretical allegiance. In the tradition of shoddy gang cryptology, You Are was a barely coded pun on the club's initials, and though wearing a You Are Here T-shirt didn't signal anything beyond desire, it might be enough to make an average civilian think twice before talking back in a crowded movie theatre, say—in the same way that a black and silver You Are Here decal on a car window would make a junkie think twice about breaking in, or might even dissuade a counter-intuitively sympathetic cop from issuing a speeding ticket.

Scott walked outside to the almost-patio that had been willed into existence when someone put tables between the café and the parking lot, and watched as the fat, muscly man climbed into a raised black truck with tinted windows, being driven by a friend. The truck's aesthetics were an inchoate and dialectical collection of elements stolen from hip hop and American redneck culture, and an unsurprising boom of rap-rock blasted from the vehicle as it gunned to life and drove away. Scott's ex-father-in-law, Darryl Chong, watched the truck take off with a smirk on his face, beeping the locks on his second-hand Audi and waving to Scott with his key. Scott waved back weakly.

Darryl Chong was among the coolest people that Scott had ever met, both in the colloquial sense of cool as well as being utterly dispassionate. At five-foot-three and a hundred and twenty pounds, he was packed, sixty-eight-year-old sinew, into black jeans and a blue golf shirt, and he nodded with his chin as he approached Scott's table.

"Hey, Scott," he said, in a Cantonese accent that somehow managed to be entirely free of musicality. "You want anything to eat or drink?"

"I'm good, I got a coffee inside."

"London Fog?"

"Yeah," Scott said.

Darryl went inside for a coconut water and came back out sipping.

"How's work?"

"Work?"

"Yeah. What are you doing for work these days?"

Scott picked a fleck of foamed milk from the side of his mouth.

"Things get pretty quiet in the summer, but I go back to tutoring once school starts again—there's, like, eight kids I work with. Their parents want their grades up for applying to schools once they graduate, so I help them with history, mostly, and a bit of English. Help them with their essays. One of them's parents wants them to practise just, whatever, like conversational English. So they pay me another hour and a half to chat with the kid."

"And that's—" Darryl started, then remembered that his daughter's well-being no longer counted in any way on Scott's professional prospects. "That's good."

"So, you been watching this shit with the Canucks?" Scott asked, trying to shift the focus of the conversation, attempting to delay any news of Michelle or any questions about the house.

Darryl briefly made a disgusted face which suggested that he had, in fact, *tasted* the Canucks. He shook his head no.

"No, Whitecaps."

"Soccer," Scott smiled. "Football, well. The person who would have loved that was my mom." Darryl smiled with half his mouth. "She loved that Michelle played. It was like a second chance. She said she was ready to coach for her grandkids."

Both men sat for a moment and wondered why Scott had fucking said that. Darryl drank his coconut water.

It had been two-and-a-half years since Michelle had tried to get Scott to come to a game, any soccer game, during their six-month backpacking honeymoon across Europe, but he had always begged off. Each of the cities they had stayed in for any serious length of time—Manchester, Rome, Istanbul—were football-crazy, but Michelle had gone alone each time. Scott had been mystified at the Turkish airport when Michelle, wearing a Galatasaray T-shirt, was cheered by half the airport security staff and booed loudly by the others, but had smiled when he saw that she, and they, were laughing.

All in all, it had been a beautiful trip, relatively affordable due to a combination of bohemian accommodations and a joblessness at home that meant that the time away came without opportunity costs. It was half a year full of sex and museums—even a few days in Belgrade at the end to visit Scott's aunts and uncles, who collected the new couple ashen-faced from the airport, full of sympathy, followed by confusion, until the realization

31

that only they knew what Bojana had been unwilling to ruin her son's honeymoon by telling him: shortly after his take-off from the Vancouver International Airport, Bojana's long-term gastrointestinal discomfort finally screeched past the point where she could bear it in her Balkan stoicism, and the doctor, very nearly angry at her, asked why she hadn't come in before the cantaloupe-sized tumour in her stomach had reached Stage IV. Bojana died while her furious and terrified son was over the Atlantic, rushing home no faster than the rest of the passengers on his plane.

Scott arrived not only to a dead mother but to a father, Peter, who had entirely collapsed. Hospital staff informed him that Peter had at one point gone two months seemingly without any sleep whatsoever and had lost as much weight as his wife, who wasn't able to eat. Although they assured him that Peter had been hysterical, sometimes to the point of needing sedation, Scott saw only a placid, loopy, peaceful version of his father when he returned. After losing his wife, he had found Christ—Christ in a particularly austere and radical, fifteenth-century German peasant Anabaptist form. The newly minted widower standing smiling in front of Scott, trying to reassure him that Bojana was sitting at God's feet, had months ago renounced all earthly, material concerns; had stopped showing up for work, was living amongst his new Brethren on a biodynamic farm in the sticks, and had allowed the house on Driftwood Crescent where Scott had grown up—that the Clark family had worked like dogs to buy from the family that had rented it to them for almost twenty years—to go into foreclosure.

It was Darryl who had stepped in and been a parent to Scott when he had had none, having lost one to cancer and another to the belief that the Ten Commandments and juicing were the only ways to fight it. Between the bit of money that Scott had inherited from Bojana's death and the liquidation of Peter's assets, he'd had half of what he needed to buy back his childhood home. Darryl supplied the rest.

But when the marriage dissolved, the clock started ticking down to Scott's two options with regards to his business partner: to buy out his half of the equity, or else to sell the property and split the take down the middle. But Josiah, in his brilliance, had outlined a third way.

"Mr Chong—"

"Scott, don't be stupid."

"Sorry. Dad—"

"Well ..."

"Darryl."

Darryl nodded.

"Darryl, I know we're closing in on the end of the year here. And I think you know—I just don't have the money to buy out your half."

"It's a very difficult market, Scott."

"It is."

"But when we sell the house, you are going to have a leg up that almost nobody your age has got. You'll be able to buy a condo practically cash."

Scott knew that if he started talking about the house, what it meant to him, which memories were living there rent-free, he would cry. But there was no need to talk about the house in sentimental terms; this was business.

"Absolutely, Darryl—I could. Or. It occurs to me that this contract, it's between you and me. There's no reason we have to do it any way but the one that's best for us. We've owned this house together for two years now, and in the course of that time, I mean, on paper—we have both made a lot of money. I know that, you know, for more than a year now, it hasn't been a home to Michelle, and I know that that was your primary motivation, helping us. And I will never forget that. But just, in purely market terms, I mean— your investment has gone up by sixty grand this past year. That's just you, your half. Together, we went up a hundred and twenty grand. In one year! The house, I mean—the house is like a tenured professor on sabbatical, for Christ's sake, it earned a hundred and twenty grand just sitting there. It's going to keep going up. And look, I know a deal's a deal. Michelle and I are divorced, and you've been incredibly gracious about the time to sort things out on my end. But look, putting all sentiment and whatever aside: there's no reason we can't keep this business relationship going. I am more than happy to have you stay on as a partner, and let's let the equity grow. I mean, there's no ceiling."

"Scott, Michelle is pregnant."

The first, instantaneous realization that Scott had when he heard the news was that he, himself, would never be a father. Beyond the idea that his ex-wife was now going to have the family that he hadn't been ready to give her, he was choked by the clear understanding that he was the end of his own family's line.

"Congratulations, Darryl. You're going to be a grandfather. A what, a *Yeh-Yeh*?"

Darryl smiled. "*Gong-Gong. Yeh-Yeh* is the paternal grandfather."

"That's amazing."

"Scott, my daughter and her new husband can't afford to stay in this city. And I can't stand the idea of being far away from my grandchild."

"No, of course."

"I'm buying them a condo. I'd rather they have a yard, a front door, but this is what I can do for them. I've done pretty well, but I don't have the cash lying around to do it without liquidating my stake in your parents' house. I'm sorry, Scott. You can still have until the end of the year, of course, but we will need to stick to the original terms."

"Of course. Of course, I understand," Scott said. And then: "Congratulations, Darryl. Honestly."

"Thank you. I'll tell Michelle you said so."

"Please."

Scott stood, leaving half of his decaffeinated London Fog, staggering through the parking lot, and driving the seven minutes home from the strip mall. Pulling in to Driftwood Crescent, the edges of the houses began to blur, a salty cloud forming at the outskirts of his vision as he sat in the driveway. Pulling the keys out of the ignition, he stared at the house, hyperventilating. Turning quickly, ashamed, his eyes lit on the NAM carved into the sidewalk. Without smiling, he pulled his cell phone from his pocket and dialled.

"Josiah?"

"This game is insane, man. I just put down a Wahhabi rebellion, and now I have to fight a bunch of anarchists."

"Do you still have your dad's old rifle?"

4

"I thought you told me he was going to kill himself."

"What do you want? Guy calls me in the middle of the afternoon, asks me for my dad's rifle. I thought he *was* going to kill himself."

"You don't have to kill yourself in Vancouver, you just wait for the housing market to do it for you."

"This is—I just can't emphasize this enough, this is an incredibly stupid idea."

"No, it isn't. Read the papers."

"Scott, he's right—this is nuts."

"Thank you."

"Why? Why is it nuts?"

"Well, for starters, nobody uses a fucking long barrel Winchester rifle for a drive-by shooting. Rifles are for hunting deer and for launching failed farmer uprisings against the British in Lower fucking Canada."

"Okay, well, for starters, the 1837 Rebellion was in both the Canadas."

"I mean, I don't think the gun is really the biggest reason this is fucked up."

"See?"

"Par, Jesus—I'm looking for your help here."

"No, I know, I am! But I just don't think that the big question here is the gun. The gun could work. It's doesn't have to be Dick Tracy—I mean, we're not using a Tommy gun to spell a message in a wall—you need what, five shots, maybe?"

"Exactly! Just enough so that the neighbours hear it. First one, two, they're going to maybe think it's firecrackers, Diwali or whatever."

"Dude, Diwali's in October."

"Whatever, you know what I mean."

"I mean, I'm here defending the rifle idea, and now you gotta say some stupid shit like people would think firecrackers going off in the middle of August was Diwali."

"So you're defending the rifle idea now?"

"I just think it's the wrong thing to emphasize, Joe. The rifle is not the problem."

"We would do it—"

"Stop saying fucking *we*, Scott!"

"We would do it when everybody's home, eight-fifteen, right in the middle of *Celebrity Dance Squad* or whatever. Crack, crack—the first two get people's attention. Prick their ears up. Two, three more—one in the car, one in the living room window, so there's something to see. Then you drive away."

"In what, my car? The car everybody sees parked over here five days a week?"

"Yeah, I mean. I don't know. You guys would probably have to steal a car."

"Okay, we're finished with this conversation. Good conspiracy, guys. Good work."

"What if we used a Car2Share?"

"Hey!"

"Pardeep, what the *fuck*? I know this is foreign to you, but can you act like an adult here for three fucking seconds and help me talk our friend out of shooting up his goddamn house?"

"It's not going to be my goddamn house anymore, Joe!"

"I'm just saying that if we used the Car2Share, nobody could ID the getaway car."

"Getaway car. Jesus."

"Just hear me out—they've got those reserved car-share spots at the mall, right? You always see them in clusters. I take one out, pick you up at your place with your dad's gun—"

"I'm not—"

"Just let him talk, fuck's sake."

"—I pick you up at your place with your dad's gun. We pull up in front of Scotty's, and you let five rounds off in what? What's realistic? Twenty seconds?"

"Thank you, Oliver Stone."

"That sounds right to me. About twenty, twenty-five seconds. People hear the first couple, they wonder what it is, they go to the window, maybe they see the last couple shots."

"Exactly. You get back in the car, rifle goes in the hockey bag, we park in a cluster at the mall, and walk back over to your car."

"And then Car2Share uses their GPS system to see which of their cars was on or near Driftwood Crescent that night."

"Oh."

"Right."

"So you rent a U-Haul."

"Jesus Christ."

"Actually that's true, though, U-Haul's old as shit. They don't have GPS. All they care about is the odometer."

"I'm serious. Par drives, Joe, you're in the back with the hatch un-locked, with the rifle. He stops, you pop out, hit the house a few times, then disappear. Tell me how that doesn't work?"

"That actually does sound pretty good," said Par. Josiah bit his lip.

"Even if we did this, *even if*, what makes you think that the story would get out that it's gang violence?"

"That's a two-step. What are the two different ways the newspapers let you know that something's gang-related, that you shouldn't worry too much?"

"Giving an Indian name seems to do the trick for most white people," said Pardeep.

"They either say 'the victim was known to police,' or else they say 'the victim is not cooperating with police.'"

"Yeah," said Josiah, with an air of admission.

"So I won't cooperate with the cops that show up."

"What's the other step?"

Scott smiled. "I get to send an email to Angelique Bryan."

"And what do you think this does, Scott?" Josiah asked. "Ultimately, I mean—what does this accomplish? What does it buy you?"

"At the very least, it sinks the property values. We get the number down to a place where we can start thinking about how to buy out Darryl's half."

"But you don't have any money, Scott. You don't have any fucking money! I mean, even if you drop the price by twenty percent, thirty percent—it's an abstraction. You don't have it."

"Fine, fine," Scott said, lurching mentally, stinging from the accurate humiliation of Josiah's assessment. "Then Darryl decides that it's not worth selling now, at the loss he'd take, and we buy some more time."

"And in the meantime," Josiah pushed, "where does Michelle live with her baby? Just to be devil's advocate here."

Pardeep looked to Scott, and Scott looked to the floor.

"Michelle's not the devil."

"I know, Scotty. That's kind of what I'm saying."

Scott stood, clearing the three glasses of water from the granite kitchen counter and into the glare of track lighting by the sink.

"I just need time, guys. There's nothing left of anything, after this house. Michelle's gone, my dad's on the fucking moon, my mom. I just need to hit pause here, catch my breath."

Josiah's breathing in the back of the U-Haul was shallow as he tried to figure out a way to hold the rifle without soaking it with his palms. Every time the truck turned, he lurched, performing dozens of balance-salvaging micro-movements to maintain his squat. He wanted to be ready to jump out without worrying about his legs going to sleep when Pardeep pounded on the back of the cabin to let him know that no one was out walking their dog, that no one would see his face, but even so, he wore sunglasses and a Mariners cap. Josiah was a Blue Jays fan, and he felt that this might grant him an added layer of deniability. He cradled the rifle in the crook of his arm as he watched the blurring sliver of pavement through the bottom of the unlocked hatch.

Sweat poured down Pardeep's back as he listened to talk-radio in an effort to numb his nerves. The panel guests had been invited on to discuss whether or not superhero blockbusters with female stars were empowering, or to what degree they were if, in fact, that answer was a given, and Pardeep had trouble keeping track of which interviewee was the English professor from the university and which guest was the pop-culture blogger. He rolled the window down for a second, then rolled it back up in case anyone recognized him. He scanned the lawns and walkways of Driftwood Crescent, and though it was a clear and beautiful evening, he was able to thump the signal for Josiah that nobody was out.

As the truck rolled to a stop, Josiah forgot how heavy the roll-down door was, that he couldn't lift it with one hand, and so he held the rifle in place with his foot as he lifted it partway, just enough to roll out, catching his Mariners visor on it and knocking the hat to the ground. As he bent to collect it, the sunglasses slid off of his face and onto the pavement, and he gathered them each with one hand and, swearing under his breath, threw them into the hold.

The first crack of the rifle shocked Josiah with its power, as guns always had despite the best efforts of his father and grandfather. By the third shot, he was squeezing more confidently, and had forgotten about even the possibility of being made by Scott's neighbours. He put bullet number four, as agreed, through the large living room window that faced onto the street, and the final round spiderwebbed the rearview window of Scott's Jetta, which Josiah only now realized was a shot they never would have taken if they'd actually been trying to kill him. Holding the rifle, Scott rolled back into the truck, pounding the side of the cargo hold to start Pardeep driving, just as the first neighbours were coming to their windows against their better judgment.

Scott had been lying on his stomach in front of the living room couch for fifteen minutes, and as the penultimate bullet punched through the window and crashed the glass frame of the Renoir print his parents had brought back years ago from Ottawa, he was sure that he could feel his heartbeat reverberating through the floor.

He hoisted himself up as the final volley went into the car, as agreed, and was overtaken with a legitimate adrenaline rush as he threw the front door open, pounding out onto the street in bare feet so that no one would think he'd been waiting, chasing after the truck with anger and manliness, as if those were different qualities, putting a show of gangster toughness on for the neighbours.

"Motherfuckers!" he screamed, trying not to smile, trying not to let the bouncing exhilaration he was feeling bubble their gang war over into obvious playacting. "Motherfuckers, I'm coming! Motherfuckers, I'm right here, you can't move me! This is my house! This is my house, motherfuckers!"

He stopped, halfway up the block, the top of his big toe ripped on the asphalt, breathing so deeply his torso looked mechanical, terrifying the neighbours whose names he still didn't know. And now, he didn't try not to smile.

"This is my motherfucking house!"

5

As he waited calmly in the kitchen for the RCMP to arrive in the wake of the shooting, Scott realized that he didn't know precisely what "not cooperating with police" meant; it was a phrase that he had heard, or read, dozens, maybe hundreds of times, a phrase around which he had built part of the edifice of his plan, but it only occurred to him as he heard the muted siren getting closer to Driftwood Crescent before reaching a shrill crescendo and a sudden killing stop that he only knew the sense of the phrase, the intention, and not any of its constitutive details. He had been perfectly relaxed until they'd arrived, but now this ambiguity plucked up the rate of his heartbeat. Did it mean refusing them access into the house? It probably didn't mean that; they could probably arrest him if he didn't let them in, couldn't they? Did it mean complete silence? When people said that so-and-so "wasn't talking to police," obviously they had to mean that so-and-so wasn't sharing anything of substance with them, right? As opposed to a blanket ban on, say, small talk? Scott worked his way through the various police procedurals he'd watched or read, mob movies, and also tried to calculate mentally what was feasible. His plan had been to let the constables knock twice when they arrived, on purpose, to keep them waiting as though he weren't playing ball, but when the time came there was no pantomime, and he sincerely kept them waiting through three sets of knocks as he formulated a plan. Breathing deeply before opening the door, Scott settled on a decision to speak more or less curtly with the officers, but that his only solid rule would be to avoid directly answering any questions.

"Hello, are you Mr Clark? Is this your house?"

Fuck.

Technically those were questions, but—did they count? I mean, what would be the point of lying about his name, or his address? Or of not answering?

"Mr Clark?"

"Yes. Yeah."

"Mr Clark, can we please enter?"

"Yes. Yeah."

The two Mounties entered the house without taking off their shoes, and for a second Scott worried that his parents would get mad before remembering that the house, for now, was his.

"Can I—" Scott started, about to offer the constables something to drink, then wondering if that was the proper etiquette even for someone who *was* planning to cooperate with police, before deciding that it certainly wouldn't qualify as a lack of cooperation. As a queasy heat vined its way from the pit of his stomach up the sides of his neck, Scott felt his knees quivering and blurted, "What seems to be the problem, officer?"

For a second, the cops seemed taken aback to hear a line of dialogue each had heard a thousand times before, in movies, but had never encountered in real life. They themselves looked like movie cops, both good-looking, both with fist-sized green eyes. The younger cop was a Middle Eastern woman, with large features on a very serious face. The older cop, a man, had impossibly thick silver hair cropped closely, and a crease running diagonally across each cheek as though his face had been carefully folded and packed for an overnight flight. When he spoke to Clark, he revealed a Québecois accent (which somehow made him seem even more like a Mountie) and a set of adult braces (which for fairly obvious reasons made him seem like less of one).

"Mr Clark, I'm Constable Gaulin, and this is Constable Sayyed," he said, passing Scott two business cards which he half-consciously took in hand before realizing that if he weren't cooperating, he probably should have refused. "We had some phone calls from some of your neighbours about gunshots and screaming. Constable Sayyed and I took a quick look around the front of your house, and it seems like there have been half a dozen shots."

"Did you have a warrant?" Scott said, needing desperately to vomit and choosing the idiocy of confrontation instead.

"I'm sorry?"

"To search the front yard?"

"Mr Clark," said Sayyed, creasing the brows of her serious face even more sternly. "We didn't have to search anything. The bullet holes in your house and car are visible from the street."

"Mr Clark, do you need to sit down?"

Scott shook his head. He could feel the plan slipping away. It was the fucking braces. They made Gaulin's handsome olive face preternaturally gentle and comforting, and they made Scott want to hug him, and maybe cry, and when he turned his attention to Sayyed, he wanted to kiss her tall, smooth forehead. He turned and looked at the broken Renoir instead.

"Mr Clark, an incident like this can be very terrifying, and shocking, and if you like, we can get an ambulance dispatched here, that's no problem."

"I'm fine."

"Mr Clark," said Sayyed, "can I ask why you didn't call us yourself after the shooting? Were you hurt, shocked?"

Scott was convinced that it was the screaming, his running after the U-Haul, the motherfuckers, that had forced the neighbours into action. He could have imagined them staying behind their curtains otherwise, telling themselves that those probably weren't gunshots—Scott could now say from experience that the first reaction to hearing gunshots is to know exactly that that was what they were, followed by the mind immediately assuring itself that it couldn't have been, that there had to be another explanation—but the screaming was too embarrassing to ignore.

Scott jutted his lower lip in response to Constable Sayyed's question.

"I didn't think it was a big deal."

"Sorry," said Gaulin. "Someone shot up the front of your house, and you didn't think it was a big deal?"

Scott turned his head away, but immediately worried that he seemed peevish, adolescent, rather than tough.

"It's nothing I can't handle myself."

"Hey, listen," Gaulin said with an authority leavened by condescending paternal concern. "This isn't hockey, Mr Clark. You're not going to get two minutes for fighting. We're the ones who'll handle this." As he spoke, his partner's face was shrivelling in confused disgust, sizing Scott up and looking as though she'd eaten the rancid sunflower seed at the bottom of the bag.

"I'm not cooperating," Scott blurted finally, shifting into high gear.

"With who?" asked Sayyed.

"With you guys, I mean. I'm not cooperating."

"I know."

"No, but, I mean officially. I—I want to enter into a, what do you call it, an official state of non-cooperation."

"Mr Clark," said Gaulin softly, "I'm going to call you an ambulance, okay?"

"Goddamn it! I just—you know when it says 'the victim is not cooperating with police'? Like in the newspaper? Just put me down for that. I'm one of those guys!"

Constable Sayyed shook her head, dumbfounded, angry, mouth agape in bewildered frustration. Gaulin spaced out, searching the room with his eyes, and landing on the broken frame on the living room floor.

"Renoir," he said.

It was Scott's turn now to peek from behind the curtains, watching as Gaulin and Sayyed made their way around the cul-de-sac, gathering what they could from the neighbours about what they had witnessed. Two hours or so after the shooting, the block was finally clear, as quiet and lifeless as on a normal, peaceful night, and Scott backed the Jetta with its spiderwebbed rear window out onto Driftwood Crescent and down the hill toward Johnson, onto Barnet Highway, hugging the side of Burnaby Mountain past the marina, past the refinery, and into North Burnaby. It had been a hot day, but now the evening air coming in from Burrard Inlet was cool, mixing with the stale heat like someone was adjusting the temperature of a bath.

Scott pulled the car off onto a side street named for a letter of the Greek alphabet and walked into a small, unfamiliar corner store where an angry looking old woman stood behind a cash register.

"Do you have internet?"

She nodded, holding up an index finger for Scott to wait, printing him off a receipt with a time code.

Scott made his way to the back of the store, where the atmosphere shifted to the distinct musk of testicles on sweatpants. A very large, ageless man with no moustache and a very long beard was breathing so loudly at one of the two computers that Scott thought that he was sleeping. The man took no notice of Scott as he sat on the stained, backless office chair next to him, shaking the mouse to wake the screen.

Occasionally casting an eye toward his aromatic, asthmatic neighbour in order to ensure privacy, Scott made his way to the Gmail homepage and registered a new account. ConcernedCitizen@gmail.com, though, was taken, as was VigilantCitizen@gmail.com, and NoCrime@gmail.com. Finally, settling on the less than poetic ConcernedCitizen12@gmail.com, he addressed a message to abryannewsblotter@vanstar.com.

Dear Ms Bryan,

Like you, I am a citizen concerned by crime. You will soon be hearing about a shooting on Driftwood Crescent in Coquitlam earlier this evening. Do not concern yourself with how I know this. Five (5) bullets were shot into the home of Scott Clark, a local THUG. It has been known for some time by those in the know that Scott is gang-affiliated. The police themselves will tell

you that he is not cooperating with police. Scott is a member of
the Non-Aligned Movement (NAM). You can even check the Dr.
Charles Best Secondary School yearbook from 2005 to see that he
was talking about it even then. Are his neighbours safe? Only time
will tell. It pains me greatly to come forward in this way, but do
we have any other choice. You are the trusted voice in crime. We
know that I can TRUST you with this delicate information.

All best,
A Concerned Citizen

The man next to Scott revved a hum of mucous in his chest, committing it to a grey handkerchief just as Scott pressed send. He logged out of the account, then cleared the browser's recent history. To be safe, he shut down the computer. Scott had three toonies in his pocket so that there would be no trace of the transaction, and on his way out the door he paid the angry old woman for fifteen minutes of internet time and a bottle of cream soda.

As he drove east along Hastings, the broad street was quiet. He rolled down his windows to fill the car with blue summer air, and accelerated when the lights were green, and slowed down when they were yellow, then red. At an intersection next to a storefront karate dōjō, a driver pulled up next to him. Her face furrowed in concern as she stared at him, and Scott blinked in confusion. Did she know about the email? He'd made certain to write it in the cadence of someone from outer space. Had she followed him from the store?

As the light turned green, the other car sped away, and only when Scott checked his rearview mirror did he see the bullet hole and the menacing cracks in the glass, and he realized that he probably shouldn't be driving the Jetta.

6

The day after the shooting, Scott met with Josiah and Pardeep at Polis, the three of them giggling over a plate of hummus and thick, cakey pita points. None of them knew what to do with the excess of adrenaline that was still pumping through each of their bodies.

"I'm ruined for *Counterinsurgency 4*," said Josiah, and all three of them had laughed.

The media from the hit had been somewhat underwhelming. There'd been no story in the print newspaper, just a short entry on Angelique Bryan's *Vancouver Star* crime blog, *The Blotter*, explaining that police were investigating a shooting on Driftwood Crescent last night, and that the victim was not cooperating. Scott had smiled with deep satisfaction when he'd seen that detail, rendered exactly as he'd seen it before in a dozen articles about gangsters. His name, though, was left out of it, as was his address, as was any of the information that Concerned Citizen had emailed to Bryan; he would have to check the account from a different corner store tonight to see if she'd responded. He would also have to call back Darryl Chong, who had phoned five or six times over the course of the day, though Scott, for the time being, ignored each call.

"So? What happens next, man?" asked Pardeep, smiling.

"Well, they didn't offer any details, so I'm going to let the broken windows sit for a little bit, make sure the word gets out. I called a realtor this morning—"

"You what?" asked Josiah.

"I called a realtor, dude," Scott said, smiling.

"Balls, bro. Balls." They laughed again.

"This guy was so cute, you could hear every one of his instincts fighting all the other ones at every turn. Trying to tell me that now wasn't the time to think about selling, but that down the line, as soon as it was, I should call him. It was perfect."

"But he said what you wanted to hear?"

Scott nodded. "Yeah, man, he said it's no good trying to sell right after something like this. You just take too big a hit."

"So you did it."

"We did it."

"Yeah, man," said Pardeep, grinning even wider. "We did it."

"I haven't decided yet how to tell Darryl. He's gonna be—I don't know if it'll be more worried, or, like, pissed, or just weirded out."

"He's never going to believe you're a gangster, though."

Scott winced slightly at how easily this dismissal came, how uncontroversially, but was too giddy to indulge his resentment. "I don't need him to. I just need a nervous realtor to tell him to wait."

As Josiah drove Scott home, the two of them laughed about the shot-up Jetta, about the audacity of what they'd done, about the neighbourhood. Josiah stopped his car outside of the house on Driftwood Crescent.

"Thanks, man."

"No sweat."

"I mean for everything."

"Actually, now that it's over—it was actually pretty fun. And I know I said it was a bad idea, but—and I mean, it was still crazy. And very stupid. But it looks like, I don't know. It looks good, man."

Scott smiled. Then he laughed.

"I told Angelique Bryan that I was with the Non-Aligned Movement. That she could check the yearbook."

"Jesus Christ!" Josiah laughed nervously. "Buddy, you're not the only one who shouted out the NAM in that yearbook."

"No, you and Par were 14-1-13, remember?"

Josiah shook his head. "That's right. Jesus, what a bunch of fucking idiots."

"I guess Adnan's fucked though."

"Wherever he is," Josiah said, raising his palms to the heavens. "Maybe this'll bring him out of hiding."

Scott smiled, staring out the window at the cul-de-sac. "I'll see you tonight? Seven-thirty?"

"Yeah. You want me to pick you up?"

"No, I'll walk. I need a change of pace."

Scott opened the front door, made his way into the kitchen, poured himself half a glass of milk, and was drinking it before he choked, seeing a man standing in his backyard.

The biker was staring off over the fence into his old yard when Scott saw him. The sight was jarringly nightmarish and surreal—he looked identical, muscles rippling out of a black T-shirt, wearing grey sweatpants, and Scott had no idea what to do when the biker looked up and saw him at the window. He moved with the smooth, terrifying grace of a Zamboni toward the back door. He didn't knock; he assumed that Scott would simply answer. Which he did.

"Hey, what's your name again?" He spoke in a voice like anybody else's, but the confidence it was filtered through made the difference. Scott was immediately on his heels.

"Uh, Scott."

"Right. I'm Mike. I own the house next door. I used to live there, you remember me?"

"Yeah, for sure. Hey, Mike."

"I'm just going to come in for a minute, okay."

It would have to be.

As he moved into the house, Mike the Biker took in the details of the room with an intensity exceeding that brought to bear by Constables Gaulin and Sayyed.

"Let's talk downstairs." Mike beckoned Scott with the side of his bald head.

"Sure. Listen, could I—"

"I'm not doing the listening today."

Scott followed Mike into the basement, suppressing a strong urge to piss or to cry, as the large man searched downstairs with a visibly increasing curiosity. He looked at the elliptical machine, then looked at Scott and almost smiled. But he didn't.

"I hear there was a shooting here last night."

"Yeah, it was—there was one, but it was no big deal."

Mike nodded understandingly, bit the side of his lower lip as he processed the information, and then lunged at Scott in one perfectly fluid and muscular motion as though he were made of lava, taking the whole side of Scott's head into his giant hand and driving it through the drywall.

There had been only two or three genuine experiences of violence in Scott's life, and each time, his immediate response had been to wonder if there was any way to go back in time in order to prevent it from happening.

But already there was nausea as Scott realized that Mike was kicking him in the ribs; that no one in the world could see them; that the only person who had the power to end what was happening was Mike himself. Too scared to cry, Scott lay dazed on his stomach as the beating stopped and Mike crouched next to him.

"What the fuck were you running out of here?"

"Nothing."

Mike knelt on Scott's back, sending a wave of excruciation through the whole circuit of his musculature. Scott's face screamed.

"What the fuck were you running?"

"Nothing, nothing. I swear."

"Why the fuck did somebody shoot up your house then, asshole?"

Scott tried to think, to speak through the cloud of pain.

"I don't know. I don't know. It was just a joke."

Mike punched Scott in the back of the leg, and Scott wondered if he would ever walk again.

"Here's the problem, Scott. I read in the fucking news that the house next to my old place, a place I still own, gets shot up, and the cunt who lives there isn't cooperating with police. So now I know something's going on in my backyard—literally, my fucking backyard—and nobody's paying me rent for it." Mike bounced Scott's head off the wall again, this time without enough purchase to make a dent in either. "This block is Riders' territory, little man. Do you understand what I'm telling you? You Are Here, bitch, because we say you are."

The hummus shot out of Scott's throat and onto the carpet at the mention of the Underground Riders. Mike was disgusted.

"Fucking bitch," he said, standing up and kicking Scott lightly in the stomach. "I should rub your fucking nose in it."

Scott struggled to sit up, trying to catch his breath as he leaned against the wall underneath the hole that had been made with his face, his body feeling like it was about to fall apart into its constitutive parts.

"Just tell me what it is. I know you're not growing down here, and there's no lab. You running bitches? A fucking card game?"

Scott shook his head. He tried to formulate the words to explain the real estate plan, but his synapses were splayed apart, each turned away from the others.

"We did it, we did it ..." was all he could manage.

Mike crouched in front of Scott, his face impassive, and slapped him hard.

"You work this block, whatever it is you're doing, you work for the Riders. It's what—it's Thursday. I'm going to be back on Sunday for your rent on whatever the shit it is you've got going, Scott. Five thousand bucks, we'll start."

"But it was just my friends who—"

Mike slapped him again, this time with his fist half-closed.

"Don't be a fucking tattle-tale, Scott."

"No! No, I wasn't. We were together. We did it—"

"It's nice being back in the old neighbourhood. I'll see you Sunday."

7

"Bro, this is ..." Pardeep trailed off. "You don't look good, Scott."

Scott moaned on the couch as he held the frozen ćevapčići to the side of his head, then, when his ribs got jealous of the cold, to his side. As he brought the sausages back up to his cheek, he could feel them softening slightly, thought he could smell them, and he thought of his mother.

Josiah came back to the couch with a look of concern on his face, wiping the freshly rinsed metal mixing bowl dry with a dishcloth.

"I don't like it, Scotty. I think we should take you to the hospital."

"I'm fine," he answered, in the precise voice of someone who wasn't. The words came through his fat lips smeared; he could taste the acid in every corner of his mouth.

"You take any kind of blow to the head, they say if you puke, you gotta go to the ER."

"I'm fine."

"It could be a concussion."

"Sidney Crosby's had fifty fucking concussions, and he's still won a million Stanley Cups even though Sidney Crosby's had fifty fucking concussions."

"Buddy, Joe's right, let's just pop down to the emergency room. Won't take more than a few hours."

"Look, check my eyes. Flash the phone."

"You're not even making any sense, Scotty."

"Goddamn it, the phone, the light—flash the phone light into my eyes, see if they dilate right. If they do, it's not a concussion. Wait, let me get them big."

Scott dropped the ćevapčići and covered his eyes with both hands, creating an artificial darkness while Pardeep and Josiah waited, sighing, hands on hips.

"Scott, buddy."

"Just let me—" Scott was cut off by the puke, his throat somehow wringing more from his stomach, somehow finding something left to heave after all these times. His hands dropped from his eyes as Josiah positioned the bowl under his chin.

"Come on, man, let's take you down to Eagle Ridge."

"I'm telling you, we'll sit there for six hours, and at the end of it they'll just tell you guys to wake me up every four hours tonight."

"Is that true?" Pardeep asked Josiah.

"I think he might be right. Unless his brain is bleeding, I think? But yeah, if it's a concussion," he said, then turned, speaking angrily toward Scott, "and it's *definitely* a concussion, there's not a ton they can do."

Pardeep and Josiah looked at each other.

"You stay with him," Josiah managed, a half second before Pardeep, who threw his hands up in surrender. Without thinking, Josiah began to smirk at his minor victory, until the sobbing started.

Scott was crying, his shoulders shuddering, a look of absolute confusion and surrender on his face.

"He's coming back," he said, rasping simultaneously at both ends of the register, low and high, resigned and shrill. "He's coming back in three days for five thousand dollars."

"Jesus."

"Fuck."

"He's going to come back, and when I don't have the money, he's going to what? He's going to kill me."

"Did he say he was going to kill you?"

"I don't know. I think it was implied."

"Scott," said Josiah, "I think it's time to call the cops."

"I don't—I'm not sure that's the right move, Joe." Josiah looked at Pardeep with as much confusion as frustration.

"Jesus Christ, Par, I can understand Scott losing his mind on this shit, but you are really starting to piss me off. If you'd had your head on earlier, you could have helped me talk him out of even starting this shit."

"You pulled the trigger, asshole!"

Josiah threw the dish towel onto the floor.

"Besides," Pardeep continued, "you're talking about ratting on the Underground Riders. That would be an iffy proposition even if the cops liked Scott, which they now have no reason to. The cops they don't own have no power to stop them."

"We don't need any of your father's conspiracy theories, Pardeep!"

"Now who's being naive!?" Pardeep screamed.

Scott's crying dropped the low end and took off into a high, sobbing shriek. Pardeep sat next to him on the couch and took his head onto his chest. The young men had never been physically affectionate with each other, and the embrace was awkward, and Josiah watched it with curiosity and a gruffly-conceded admiration, wondering if that's how he would have hugged Scott if he'd had to.

"Scott, what kind of cash do you have on hand?" Pardeep asked. "I think we give him the money on Sunday, I don't see any way out of that. And it's a token, it's a gesture of whatever. Good fate."

"Faith," said Josiah.

"You'll give him an envelope with the money he asked for, and then you can explain that the shooting was a set-up. That there was nothing really going on. He's up five grand, no harm, no foul."

Scott ran his fingers over the goose egg growing from his head as he tried to sort out this particular usage of *no foul*.

"I don't have five thousand dollars, Par."

"What do you have?"

"Nothing."

The men sat in silence for a few seconds. Josiah made pleading eye contact with Pardeep, who shook his head with gentle helplessness.

"I just bought plane tickets for my mom. India, at Christmastime. I'm tapped."

Josiah shrugged preemptively.

"I literally haven't had a savings account since I started my master's."

For a moment, the acute panic of their immediate circumstances gave way to a general mourning of their long-term predicament, as three purportedly middle-class men in their early thirties who, between them, had nothing close to five thousand dollars. Mike may as well have been coming back for a bag of rubies.

Pardeep had planned to sleep next to Scott in his parents' old queen-size bed, setting two alarms four hours apart from each other, but when the time came he couldn't close his eyes. As Scott snored gently, punctuated by an occasional moan, Pardeep tried to keep himself busy, looking for books or magazines, finding one of Scott's father's religious pamphlets instead, and sitting with it for a few minutes.

We are each of us Sinners, and in that Sin we are BELOVED

Beneath the banner was a pixelated reproduction of a painting of three hillside crosses, captioned *Christ and the two Thieves*.

Pardeep smiled condescendingly. He wasn't particularly religious himself, but found Christianity's meekness to be especially, endearingly odd. He thought about the physical courage embodied in Sikhism, how much it had appealed to him and to the other young boys at the *Gurdwara* when he was growing up, and he wondered what little Christian boys thrilled to, fantasized about. He wondered if that was why they had grown up to be such assholes all over the world, as compensation. He thought about the naughty jokes that Bojana had made about the Pope while they were growing up, how she would make them giggle conspiratorially and how much they all liked to watch her laugh, how her eyes would close and her chest would shake, and how the former offered a teenaged boy the chance to appreciate the latter. One night, during a sleepover, when Scott had left the room to find chips, Pardeep, Josiah, and Adnan had quickly and quietly confided in each other their shared admiration of Bojana Clark, and Pardeep had gone to bed laughing silently but woke in horror to a stickiness inside the sleeping bag he had borrowed from his host. After encouraging the other boys to go ahead to breakfast without him, that he would lazily make his way down, he had run to the bathroom for a towel and was crouched over the sleeping bag on the floor of Scott's room trying desperately and unsuccessfully to wipe it, to prevent the spreading stain from attaining any greater visibility than it already had on the bright blue nylon, when Bojana had walked in.

"Pardeep, you eat enough of my food that you can start doing chores. This is not Yugoslavia. Here, everyone has to actually earn their stay. Take those sleeping bags down to the laundry and put them in the washer, will you?" She had asked loudly enough that even in the kitchen, the other boys could hear.

Pardeep had thought that he'd won the lottery; that he was the luckiest kid in Coquitlam. It wasn't until years later, when all four members of the Non-Aligned Movement were going for their post-graduation hunting trip, that he understood what had actually happened. Bojana and Peter had been kind to the boys, not pointing out that an all-male camping trip was so evidently a nerd's way out of not having been invited to any of the sex-riddled graduation parties that would be happening in town. Bojana had allowed herself just one ironic remark while the boys were loading the van.

"Oh, Scott—are you sure you want Pardeep using your sleeping bag?"

No one else had noticed, but Pardeep, his cheeks mauve, had whipped up to see Bojana looking at him, the olive flesh in the vee of her black sweater dimpled and soft, and she winked. Pardeep giggled as he realized that not only had Bojana known exactly what was going on, not only had she saved him his dignity without missing a beat or making a big deal of it—he also became convinced, against all reason and common sense, that she'd known he was dreaming about her.

Pardeep's cellphone began clanging on the nightstand, and he reached over to turn it off before looking at Scott, looking at the pamphlet, and doing one last equation in his head. He shook his friend on the shoulder.

"Scotty? Scotty?"

Scott sat up in slow motion.

"Yeah?"

"You still alive, *gora?*"

"I gotta go to the bathroom."

Pardeep didn't smile as he watched Scott leave the room, heard him make his way down the hallway to the bathroom, heard him take a short piss and, without flushing, run the sink only long enough to fill a glass of water. Pardeep shook his head, preemptively regretting his own decision.

Scott walked back into the bedroom.

"I feel better. Do I look any better?"

"No, Scott. *You* look like a plate of moussaka."

"At least it's better than lasagne."

"Scott, I—" Pardeep bit his lip, then sucked his teeth. "I think I know where you can get your hands on the cash for Sunday."

"What? Where?" Scott said, the first notes of hope entering his voice since the beating.

The hope went out of his face as Pardeep outlined the ways in which his father's suspicion of credit and debit cards would leave the till at Polis flush with cash every week, and the back room too, with tabs from Thursday, Friday, and then Saturday nights. He shook his head in refusal as Pardeep explained that his parents had left for Harrison Hot Springs for the weekend, that he would be managing the restaurant Saturday night and so no one would be traumatized; that in a few months, they could return the loan without any big fanfare.

"Par, I can't do that. I love your parents. I love Polis."

"That's fine. And my parents, and Polis, are going to be okay. There will be several thousand dollars for the taking, and nobody will be hurt. Scott, Joe was right—I should've helped him talk you out of all this. I got sentimental about this place, though, just like you. And so now I got to help get you out of it."

"We could—"

"What?"

"I mean, I'm just thinking. If we do the robbery, we could say it was the Non-Aligned Movement. Spread the rumour. Help bolster the story. Unless—your dad doesn't know about NAM, does he?"

"Not a thing. I did 14-1-13, remember?"

"That's right. Okay. But what if we get caught?"

"Who's going to catch you? I'm the one being robbed. I mean, my dad's got webcams behind the counter, so you couldn't show your faces. But there's no sound, though, just pictures. We should be fine."

"Pardeep, I can't. I mean—couldn't we just ask your parents? If the money's there?"

Pardeep dropped his head. "I can't explain this to them over the phone. Besides, man, you know my dad—if we take this to him before it's solved, he'll want to put himself in the middle of it. Big tough guy, take all those bikers down single-handed."

Scott shook his head. "I can't ask you to do this to your family."

Pardeep looked at Scott, angry that he was forcing him into a position of sentimentality.

"You're family too, you dumb *gora*."

8 .

The Canadian spoke with a sort of hybridized accent such that the British could never place him regionally or socio-economically, and so none of them were ever comfortable with him off the bat. He was from all over the place, which meant in a way that he was from nowhere, or at least that he wasn't from any place which they knew instinctively was better, or worse, than where they were from. He never talked politics or religion with anyone, never talked football, and so the many people that the Canadian did business with had learned not to try to make small talk.

The truck driver was fine with that; if he wanted to bullshit with co-workers he could have taken a job in a call centre or a pub. He appreciated that he and the Canadian could share quick, terse nods as he came around from the cab, having backed into the loading bay of the Canadian's warehouse in the middle of the night. He was alone, standing on the lip of the empty loading dock, next to the one that they were using, wearing the three-piece suit of a CIA funeral director, only cut perfectly.

The driver said "You're all right?" and the man nodded, eyes closed briefly, as though he were embarrassed that they had to waste their time even with that. The driver broke the seal, hoisting open the back of the trailer, and to his credit, as he always did, the Canadian came in with him and rolled the racks out.

"Mind if I use the toilet while you count?"

The Canadian nodded, his finger already crooked and pecking through the air, taking inventory.

It was a long piss; the driver had been in the cab since the dock, just after nightfall, and would now be turning right back around. When he came out of the toilet, the Canadian had finished his count, and had the usual two bags ready for him—one large, one small.

"Ta," said the driver.

"No, thank you."

The Canadian winced as the truck pulled off noisily into the cool summer darkness, shutting each of the loading bay doors remotely as he headed back to the new racks, taking the end of a sleeve between his thumb and forefinger. It looked exactly right. Poring over them, he could see that they all did. He allowed himself a smile.

The racks were filled with strong, dark, solid colours, but each rack also held three pinstriped suits, spaced out among the others. He took one of these, now, at the shoulder, and ran his hand up the lining.

The Canadian smiled.

Angelique Bryan was nearing the end of her day at the *Vancouver Star* offices and hadn't yet had time to go over the international wire stories. She checked the clock and wondered if she could put it off until tomorrow. Angelique had seen more than half of her co-workers over the years marched out of the death-rattling newspaper with buy-outs in hand, and it always meant that there was that much more to do, in an office that was that much less fun to be in. The glamour of the office had been in decline for decades, but in the rearview mirror, the Golden Age kept getting paradoxically closer. Five years ago, things had felt austere—but today, five years ago seemed like Old Hollywood, with unlimited budgets and bacchanalian Christmas parties, not to mention city council coverage and a theatre reviewer. Nowadays, Angelique was not only responsible for investigating and reporting her own local crime stories and posting at least one *Blotter* blog entry per day, but they also wanted a law-and-order column every two weeks, along with profile-raising panel appearances and interviews on local television and radio news broadcasts, which were as awkward as they were unpaid, which was to say entirely—and now, on top of all that, she was also meant to troll the waters of international crime stories, looking for the weird or salacious, rewriting whenever possible with a local hook, however it could be crammed in. She had too much pride to do the jobs poorly and was now averaging a seventy-hour week. Her ex-husband had gone back to Toronto.

Cecil had never understood how she could stand to live in a city so white.

"It's not white," she'd say. "It's just, I don't know, *not Black.*"

"Exactly what I said."

Cecil had tried for years to get her to move with him to Toronto, where there was a community, he pleaded—where there were entire blocks and entire streets where they could breathe easier. Shit, even his landlord was Black back home. They could have ackee and saltfish without having to plan a special trip to the suburbs.

"I grew up in Vancouver," she would tell him. "We have a community out here."

"You and a painting of Jimi Hendrix—that's not a community, girl. And the rest of the world says Jimi's from Seattle." Angelique had loved his soft Jamaican accent—her own roots were Grenadan and Haitian, but she had grown up on music from Jamaica—and was willing to forgive even this blasphemy about Hendrix.

"He's from both. A man can be from more than one place."

But as the newsroom thinned and Angelique's workweek bloated, the pressures of a damp and beige city compounded the strain, and now she was alone again. Forty-seven years old, and though she had no worries about her face or her body—no problems at all making a good impression, even on the very young men she caught looking or asking her out over Twitter, boys of all colours—there wasn't much a woman could do with half an hour a week not spent working or sleeping.

Angelique sighed long, officially excusing herself from the wire stories until tomorrow. She should, though, follow up on the weird email, even if it was foolishness. Nothing about it worked: for starters, who in the hell was ConcernedCitizen12? Why was their email so strangely worded? If this Scott Clark was gang-affiliated, how had she never heard of him? The yearbook story, at least, checked out. Angelique had convinced a tanned and reluctant principal to let her into the school, for now emptied by the season, to retrieve a copy of the annual. Clark had named the NAM in his graduation write-up; there'd been one other boy, too—an Adnan abd-Husseini, whom she couldn't find anything about online, but who didn't look any more crooked than Clark. They seemed like sweet, nerdy boys. But his house had been shot up, and she had received a tip, and even though dinner time was ninety minutes ago, Angelique supposed that she had to make an effort to follow up, and that now was just as good a time as any other, which would also be terrible.

The only number she had was for the landline associated with the address. She dialled, hoping that she wouldn't have to have the conversation as she heard the fourth ring, but then, like so many women before her, her hopes for a relaxing evening were dashed by the sound of a man's voice.

"Hello?"

"Hello, is this Mr Scott Clark?"

"Speaking."

Angelique thought he sounded shaky, maybe sick.

"Mr Clark, this is Angelique Bryan, from the *Vancouver Star*. I was wondering if we might talk for a minute?"

He took a few seconds, and then: "Yeah. Yeah, for sure."

He sounded better now, very suddenly; Angelique was fairly certain that she could hear him smiling.

"I was hoping to speak to you about the shooting at your home, Mr Clark, and what it might relate to."

"Yeah. Absolutely."

"... And, so?"

"Oh, sorry. You mean now?"

"Would there be a better time?"

Now she could hear him thinking; when he came back on the line, he had shaken the boyish enthusiasm from his voice. He had hardened.

"I'm not going on the record. I can't give you anything, for, uh ... like, a quote ..."

"Attribution?"

"Yeah, I can't say anything for attribution. I have business relationships and business arrangements that would be very sensitive to attribution."

"I see."

"And I don't really feel comfortable doing this on the phone."

Angelique immediately began running a host of mental calculations, taking measurements and making odds, sussing out the level of risk posed by Scott Clark. She had a strong instinct that he wasn't for real, but anything was possible in this town, and there were a great many men from the Vancouver underworld who would appreciate a crack at Angelique Bryan in a position of vulnerability.

"What do you have in mind then?" she asked finally.

"Could you—meet me at Rocky Point Park, over by the kids' playground, Sunday afternoon? Say, three o'clock?"

Good God Almighty, Angelique thought has she shook her head in resignation, watching the last little bit of her week break off into the ocean like an irretrievable piece of the Antarctic.

"Yes, I can do that, that's fine. If anything comes up before then, is this the best number to reach you at?"

"Actually, no. This was my parents' line. I really don't use it."

"Your parents?"

"This used to be their house. Let me give you my cell?"

Angelique took down the number in the corner of her notebook.

"How will I know you?" she asked. The boy would be thirteen years off his grade twelve yearbook photo.

"I'll know you," he said, then took a deep breath. "You're very ...

you're quite stunning, Ms Bryan. Your picture in the paper, what do you call that, the like, pencil drawing of you?"

"It's called a hedcut," she said, pointedly not thanking him for the compliment. "I'll see you Sunday."

9

"Have you noticed how there's been a slippage, lately, in the use of the term 'single parent'?"

"What?"

"'Single parent,' I've just—you hear it a lot now, and people just use it to mean they're divorced."

"So what?"

"I mean, that's 'co-parenting,' isn't it? For me, 'single parent' means the other parent is out of the picture entirely; either they're dead or they've abandoned the situation somehow. Jail maybe—the other parent's in jail. But calling yourself a 'single parent' if you get every other weekend off, couple evenings free every week—I just, I don't know—that seems self-congratulatory to me."

"Scott, nobody fucking gives a shit. It doesn't matter."

"Jesus, sorry. I was just making an observation, man."

"No, what you're trying to do is to pretend that this is a normal, alright thing. That this is just us, doing something. And it isn't. This is fucked up to all hell."

Polis had been the only thing they'd had as teenagers, the only bit of social capital that they'd been able to cling to in an impossible high school ecosystem of ego, hormones, cruelty, and non-stop eating. Just off of North Road, in the neighbourhood of Burquitlam—perhaps the ugliest neologism in the annals of global city planning; a portmanteau of "Burnaby" and "Coquitlam" so simple and grotesque as to suggest that it had been named by someone in the midst of having a stroke—the restaurant drew the kids from their school like insecure, impossibly judgmental flies, and the claim that the NAM boys had to the place made them visible in a way that they never were in class or in the hallways. Pardeep, as the sole front-of-house staff during non-school hours, ran Polis like a *seigneurie*, assigning tables, determining whether it was the swaggering boys from the football team or the regal boys from the golf team who got to sit near the group of cheerleaders sharing a plate of chicken souvlaki; it was Pardeep who determined who got prime real estate next to the windows where they could be seen at the centre of the action, and who sat next to the bathroom where legumes and semi-exotic spices were processed by immature gastrointestinal tracts. And if Scott, Josiah, and Adnan were nobodies in the Charles Best cafeteria, at Polis they were three Ray Liottas as three Henry Hills, escorted lovingly to the best seats in the house.

The four of them had celebrated Josiah's sixteenth birthday after hours at the empty bar, making their way through an entire bottle of ouzo stolen from the glass shelf filled with liquor bottles. Adnan had been particularly eager to prove that Muslims could drink, guzzling straight from the bottle while the boys sang "Ouzo like Sunday morning ..." until he blacked out in one of the booths. All four of them had been so galactically sick the next day, and Gurdeep so infuriated about the theft, that although he himself had long since vowed never to raise his hands against his son, he drove Pardeep to the home of his grandfather, Bahadur, who had no such compunction, and who delivered several quick slaps and boxings about the ears.

But tonight, it was as though Scott were seeing Polis for the very first time, as a new and strange place. As a party of three laughing, middle-aged women carrying already-greasy leftover boxes left through the front door, Pardeep had extinguished the orange-and-blue of the neon OPEN sign, which was the agreed-upon signal that the last of the patrons in the dining area and the last family members in the kitchen had finally gone home, leaving him alone with the money, vulnerable to brigands. The large sign over the awning—POLIS: AN AUTHENTIC HELLENIC DINING EXPERIENCE— had always made the boys laugh, especially the way that Gurdeep would try half-heartedly to defend its honesty, smirking only a little as he explained that Alexander the Great had made it all the way to India, that it was a shared heritage, if only tenuously.

Tonight the sign looked dingy, somehow unreal. Having passed underneath it an impossible number of times, tonight Scott found it to be unfamiliar.

More familiar, though, was Darryl Chong's name flashing up, again, on his phone. Scott sighed, staring for another moment out the window, before finally giving Darryl something.

Darryl I'm sorry. I can't talk now but promise to reach out soon. I am okay. The house is going to be okay. I promise to call when I can.

"Are you ready?" Josiah was seething, and Scott could neither blame nor comfort him. He did his best to telegraph contrition and gratitude, but his face still badly bruised and swollen, he had no sense of what he looked like and whether or not the emotions were getting across.

"Josiah—"

"Can we just do it? Can we just fucking get this over with so I can put this gun down and never pick it up again?" Josiah had been vociferously opposed to the plan from the moment Pardeep presented it, but he had also been hurt by Pardeep's suggestion that it was none of his business, ultimately, and he seemed legitimately heartbroken by Scott's insistence that, if necessary, he would do the stick-up by himself.

"It's not really a stick-up, just remember that," Scott said, as much picking up the thread of his own private thoughts as he was reassuring Josiah. "The show is just for the webcams, nobody is in there who's gonna be scared. I'll sell the Jetta, I'll do something—in a couple weeks I'll get the Dhaliwals their money back. Joe, I promise. This is the end of it."

Scott's phone buzzed back:

???

Josiah shook his head and spat, wordlessly throwing a balaclava into Scott's chest, and they both pulled them on.

As though he were doing *commedia dell'arte*, the mask transformed Josiah's mood and character completely, and suddenly he was giddy, barely able to contain himself. The two friends stood giggling idiotically at each other over the open trunk, hugging each other before Josiah hoisted the rifle for the last time and nodded.

A trill of anonymity shot through every part of Scott as he entered the space a stranger now, Pardeep convincingly throwing his hands up in brilliant terror, a performance that spurred a new commitment to realism from Josiah and Scott.

"Grab a fucking paper bag and empty the till, motherfucker!" Scott shouted, feeling the artificial fibres of the balaclava rubbing against his open wounds in a slight chemical throb. His hands were empty, so he clenched and unclenched his fists, grabbing a napkin dispenser and hurling it against the wall. Pardeep's eyes followed the napkins to the wall, and his response was the worst one imaginable.

He began to laugh.

Pardeep looked at Scott and Josiah helplessly, tears of laughter streaming down his face, desperately trying to signal them that he couldn't stop. Scott felt a swell of laughter bubbling up in his own throat, tried desperately to swallow it. The webcams wouldn't be able to hear Pardeep's giggling— they might see his shoulders shaking, but he could always pass that off as crying, if he had to, though he'd likely never live that down with Gurdeep. If Scott broke up, though, then the Dhaliwals would be able to tell something was going on. But he couldn't help it. Here was one of his two best friends in the world, whom he'd known for as long as anyone could, and they were pantomiming this cops-and-robbers ridiculousness and the love and the nerves were too much, and he covered his mouth.

Few things shut down a fit of laughter more viciously than a rifle shot.

The bottles behind Pardeep's head exploded, and he and Scott turned to Josiah in genuine terror.

"You fuckers got me into this, and you're not going to fuck it up giggling like a couple of stupid kids. Empty the fucking till and take us into the back for more. Move."

Pardeep nodded, filled with a rush of shamed solemnity, filling a paper bag with everything in the till. Josiah moved to a position at the door to the kitchen, staying within view of the webcam, letting Scott follow Pardeep back to where the rest of the money was. Nearly seven thousand dollars—it was more than even Pardeep had been expecting.

"I only need five."

"Scott, would you think for ten seconds? How am I going to explain to them that you didn't take it all?"

Scott nodded, stupidly, hoisting two large, brown take-out bags full of cash under his arms. He backed out of the kitchen, past Josiah, who backed out in his turn, lowering the gun as he left through the front door, and running with Scott toward the car.

Pardeep breathed deeply, poured himself a cup of tea, and waited until he could hear the car start and pull away before he called 9-1-1, asked for police, reported that there had been a robbery, that he wasn't injured, and that yes, he would wait until officers and paramedics arrived. Then he called his father's phone.

"*Hanji?*"

"Daddyji? We've been robbed."

Pardeep could hear his father drop the phone for a second, swearing quietly, desperately.

"Dad? Did you hear what I said? We've been robbed."

"No," Gurdeep said. "We haven't."

Eclipse Billiards in West Burnaby sounded identical to half the pool halls in the world, and fairly similar to the other half. There are only two ways that a pool hall can sound: either it was just the pearly crack of the balls colliding on felt—paradoxically fragile and solid in a way that made it somehow surprising that they weren't chipped or filled with divots afterwards—coupled with the murmurs of men assenting to or dissenting from the quality of shots; or else, on the other hand, it was all those sounds over a bed of aesthetically unchallenging music. Tonight at Eclipse, there was a CD of Billy Joel's *Greatest Hits*, celebrating the oeuvre of an artist suited almost perfectly to the greatest hits album as an artistic form. Wayne Brosh, Underground Riders associate, tried to find a mental air pocket of nostalgia in the lyrics to "The River of Dreams" as he pulled his cue back and snapped it forward into the break, sinking two solids and, unfortunately, a stripe. There was no avoiding collateral damage.

Wayne's father, Don, had started taking him to play pool when he was about seven years old, a series of Saturday afternoons that had felt like a tradition at the time but probably didn't last more than a few months altogether. Don was proud of how old-school it was, the way it brushed the Brosh boys up against an unseemly social element for a few controlled hours—"There's plenty of greasers in there, but we don't mind. We just play pool," Don had explained to his in-laws at a family gathering, bragging about Wayne's preternatural ability. A few years later, Wayne and Don would argue about whether or not the family should get their own table, for downstairs. By that time, Don had stopped bragging to anyone about Wayne. He never wondered if the proximity to greasers on those consecutive Saturday afternoons had turned his son into what he'd become; instead, he bitterly searched the mental archives of his wife's parenting, sometimes even his own, looking for what had to be the singular explanation for his son's turn to thuggery.

Nevertheless, Wayne, who was not typically described as being a grateful man, was at some brooding, silent level of the cul-de-sac nihilism of his personality, thankful that Don had taught him the basics. There were various endeavours—sports, games, skills—at which masculine accomplishment was judged on the spot, across the full spectrum of mannish social behaviour: sexless geeks cared about how you played chess; if you couldn't play cards, a guy from Hong Kong wouldn't consider you for a second; and tough white men expected you to be able to chase balls into pockets, with no recourse to bitch-sticks or asses on the tables.

Wayne had played all through high school; they'd started bringing girls at one point, and they'd giggled like bubbling poison when Eric Lapointe had tried to convince Allison Foner, with that universally coveted bum and those jeans without pockets, that the proper shooting position was practically folded over the side of the table. Eric was in Regina now, a city something like the suburbs where they'd grown up, in that it was somehow boring and menacing at the same time.

Wayne sank the four-ball in the side pocket, and Paul "Frenchie" Mouffe—who was full-patch, and so who couldn't be mocked either for losing or for being named "Mouffe"—let a bicultural "*Calice* fuck" hiss out through his teeth. Wayne smiled with his chin, halfway apologizing for his skill, chalked his cue, then drew a line of blue chalk from the end of the stick onto the space between his thumb and his index finger. This last step marked too much preparation for Frenchie's liking.

"Away, *sacrément*," said Frenchie. "Quit covering your goddamn hands like a savage. Stop wasting time! You get chalk all over your hand, and your balls will be blue when you fuck it, *tapette*."

One of the other Riders had told Wayne that "*tapette*" was Québec for "faggot," and so now he had to hold himself up against it in just such a way that showed sufficient respect for the patch without offering his belly to the insult.

"I don't play that *tapette* shit, Frenchie."

"Ah, *oui*?" Frenchie smiled.

"I sink balls in just two places: in gash and on felt." He knocked the two-ball into the corner. "I learned how to do both in basements."

Frenchie smiled contritely, and the green light in front of his face burst to pieces.

Bullets were entering the pool hall at a rate illegal in Canada; there were no firearms in the country smiled upon benignly by the forces of law enforcement that discharged rounds with such Yankee alacrity. The large front windows, painted remedially with a full set of racked balls, shattered in a perfect break. A few of the girlfriends in tow let loose screams, and Frenchie was barking orders to hit the floor as he dove into the shards of broken green lamp that had just been hanging over the now-darkened table.

Wayne went down onto the palms of his hands, rolling under the table that had been behind him. Flakes of chipped paint of all colours, solids and stripes, rained down onto the floor as he reached for the revolver he'd had tucked into the back of his waistband; the piece he'd learned to play without being distracted by, learning no longer to pay it any mind. He cocked the hammer as the rain of bullets slowed, then stopped, and took a deep breath. Once it had been more than two or three seconds between rounds, Wayne rolled out again and stood, both hands squeezing the gun, emptying six bullets uselessly out into the night.

As a car screeched unseen out of the parking lot, Wayne rushed to help those who hadn't yet stood; he brushed the glass out of Frenchie's hair, guided weeping girlfriends into the arms of their Riders. After three, then four, then five incredulous head counts, there were defiant whoops at the lack of casualties.

Wayne Brosh was grateful.

10

Angelique pulled into the dry, dusty lot at Rocky Point Park already feeling pissy at having been reminded that Rehanah's was closed on Sundays. The chance of picking up the singular worthwhile goat roti west of—what, Toronto?—had loomed as the only possible silver lining to this day-off work trip into the suburbs, meeting with the man ConcernedCitizen12 seemed convinced was a gangland mastermind but on whom Angelique couldn't otherwise seem to get a bead one way or the other. Even Cecil, when he'd been in Vancouver, would stop complaining when they'd make the trip out to Rehanah's, besides occasional grumblings that Jamaican roti was better than Trini roti, but Angelique always thought those were pro forma. Owing to the quality of her product and the paucity of competition for it, Rehanah had never had to develop the solicitous, pandering Starbucks approach to customer service; she closed when the kitchen was empty, she took catering jobs in the middle of regular store hours, and to Angelique and Cecil's un-ending delight, she steadfastly refused to serve full-spice dishes to anyone who hadn't eaten there before and so didn't know what they were in for.

Instead, Angelique smacked the taste of an unremarkable chicken taco salad from the sides of her mouth as she replaced her glasses with prescription shades, taking a quick look in the rearview mirror to see if she lived up to her hedcut. She shook her head in irritation, thinking of the friends who had invited her to join them at the Car-Free Street Festival in the city, whom she'd had to turn down, once again, despite realizing that she hadn't seen them since spring.

The scanner had been alive last night, a summertime Saturday evening, leaving a great deal of writing to do for Monday. The downtown fireworks display hadn't disappointed, or more accurately didn't fail to disappoint—offering up the usual knife-wielding idiocy and brutish street-fighting, casual gay-bashing, and littering that seemed inevitable whenever the city turned its central urban beach into a nightclub for suburban kids. There'd been a higher than average number of auto thefts, suggesting that some people were anticipating Car-Free Day with Free-Car Night. There had been a hold-up at a beloved Burquitlam Greek restaurant, followed by another stilted email from ConcernedCitizen12 pointing the finger at Scott Clark and the Non-Aligned Movement; most significantly, there had been a miraculously fatality-free shooting at a Burnaby pool hall, Eclipse Billiards, crawling with Underground Riders and their associates, but since no one had been injured, let alone killed, it seemed reasonable to assume that the other shoe set dangling by the Tam and Miller killings had yet to drop.

The RCMP had held a press conference that morning, typically unthinkable on a Sunday, but the violence had now frothed over from typical, and the Vancouver suburbs seemed to be in something like a state of emergency. This wasn't a private booze can or some gangster's cash-washing strip club that had been shot up, but a public pool hall where the children of actual voters could have been playing.

The police had struck a note of avuncular consternation in their statement—not anger so much as disappointment—and concluded with a plea for information from anyone who might have any, which seemed unlikely even to them. The B-teams of various television newscasts, low-seniority reporters and videographers who could be forced to work on the Sabbath, gathered precious footage for evening broadcasts and embedded content for online stories. This was no way to spend a weekend.

A couple of kids ran in front of Angelique screaming, dousing each other with water.

"Logan! Olivia! Pay attention to your surroundings!" their father called after them, smiling apologetically at Angelique and shrugging his bright pink shoulders. Angelique smiled understandingly, offering absolution, when the young father squinted through his shades. "Do I know you from somewhere?"

"Pam Grier," Angelique said, which wasn't entirely fair—he could very well be a *Star* subscriber, or have seen her on the local news—but that taco salad had left her feeling as cold and unloving as its iceberg lettuce.

Angelique was as mystified as anyone else as to why or how the peace between the Da Silvas and the UR had come apart. Broadly speaking, the bikers were retailers for the Mafia in central Canada, while the Da Silvas brought product in from the Hong Kong triads. Everyone sold a little of everything, but the peace had come through a broad, flexible understanding that coke from back east would be the Riders' general focus, while heroin from the Far East—in exactly the opposite direction from back east—would be the staple for the Da Silvas. Everybody sold pot, but that was essentially limitless and local, and more or less legal, and since their southerly neighbours in Washington had decriminalized the drug, neutralizing the profitability of border-hopping, it wasn't of the same competitive concern anymore.

Angelique had heard unconfirmed stories that the Da Silvas had discovered the joys of Mexican cocaine, or that cartel meth was performing its own Silicon Valley-style market disruption, bringing with it the creative destruction so beloved by believers in capitalist dynamism. But the Da Silva–UR peace had been so hard-won, had come after so many bodies and arrests and Angelique's National Magazine Award, that it seemed unlikely that new, Mexican business wouldn't just have been absorbed into the old arrangement.

There was another persistent rumour that felt too stupid not to have at least a kernel of truth to it: that, like a Kitsilano hippie commune of old, the gang truce had been undone by an episode of polyamory gone wrong. The story that Angelique had heard from multiple sources—and every time, she nearly lost her bottom mandible, so slack was her jaw from the sheer masculine idiocy of the tale—was that over the May long weekend at a Riders' party in Kelowna, the now-deceased Wayson Tam had cooperatively fucked a becoming young stripper named Shannon with a full-patch Rider named Ashley "Meat Pete" Peters. Meat Pete, as suggested by his sobriquet, had made his first money in pornographic endeavours, specializing in hiring recent Lower Mainland film school graduates who knew their ways around lights, sets, and cameras, but who had emerged from their serious contemplations of Sofia Coppola and Wong Kar-wai to find that work wasn't readily available, besides making crotch-shots for Meat Pete. Given his past artistic undertakings, Meat Pete was known as a particularly libertine partygoer, pursuing pleasure more fluidly than, say, Wayson Tam, who had apparently been initially put off by the ratio of the proposed threesome but had soon come around.

According to observers, the fun with Shannon had happened on a Friday, had seemed to be forgotten by Saturday, but drunkenly reasserted itself as a topic of conversation on Sunday afternoon, as Meat Pete—some would say defensively—began expounding upon the enormous size of Wayson Tam's contribution. Good-natured laughter ensued; a geographically inevitable reference to Ogopogo was made; Wayson had winced, though not bucked, at least at first, against the unoriginal and racially questionable nickname "Long Dong Tam."

As the conversation continued, though, word had it that Wayson began chafing at the easy back-and-forth about sexual escapades that, whoever else they included, or however little contact there had been between them, had technically involved another man. By late Sunday night, Tam had smashed a bocce ball into the side of Meat Pete's jaw, and though the story was too inconceivably moronic to be the cause of discord and disruption to a multi-million dollar industry, the timelines between the Victoria Day ménage à trois and the unravelling of the truce did line up.

Fucking *idiots*.

"Ms Bryan?"

There was a sweetness in Scott Clark's voice that Angelique hadn't noticed over the phone, and as she turned to see who had called her she suppressed a maternal gasp at the cuts, bruises, and scabs on his face.

"Scott?"

He nodded.

"Do you want something to drink or anything?" Scott asked her, pointing toward the concession.

"No, thank you," Angelique said, for the first time finding the young man's crush a little bit endearing, from underneath the lacerations. "Can I ask, what happened to you?"

Scott gently waved away her concern.

"It's all in the game, I guess," he answered, giggling a little bit, which seemed to make things even fishier. "What did you want to see me about?"

"I wanted to contact you for your side of the story about the shooting at your home, and your refusal to cooperate with police. I also wanted to get your thoughts about the accuracy, or inaccuracy, of an anonymous tip that I received about you."

"Anonymous tip?" Scott asked, making a too-impressed face.

"I have to say, it seemed bogus to me."

"What did it say?" he said, seriously now.

"Are you part of an organization called the Non-Aligned Movement?"

Scott bit his swollen lip.

"I can't offer any comment on that."

"So you don't deny either the existence of the Non-Aligned Movement or your membership in it?"

"This is—is this for attribution? Is it, like, on the record?"

"It doesn't have to be. We're talking."

Scott chewed his thumbnail, staring into the middle distance while Angelique wondered if she was wasting her weekend.

"Listen, as long as you don't say it was me confirming anything?"

"I don't like to do it, but with good enough reason I can cite an anonymous source."

"The Non-Aligned Movement is real. I'm one of the founders."

Angelique arched an eyebrow, making a note despite herself. None of it seemed right: the chubby thirty-something she'd never heard of as a player, this boy with a soft look whose name had never otherwise come up—and if he were for real, why did he want her to know? Was he using her as a megaphone? Making a name for the NAM?

"Who shot up your house?"

"Enemies."

"Well ..."

"Sorry?"

"I didn't think it was friends."

Scott smiled.

"What about the stick-up last night at the Greek restaurant?"

Scott nodded. "What about it?"

"I've heard rumours that that was the Non-Aligned Movement, too."

"Yeah? Where'd you hear that?"

"Same source that brought the Non-Aligned Movement to my attention in the first place."

"Hm," Scott offered, nodding with a satisfied pout, pretending at distraction.

"Is that a yes? A no?" Angelique asked, growing impatient.

"Lots of stuff happens, I don't know. It's a big city."

"Coquitlam?"

"Listen, I feel like I owe you an apology," he said.

"I'm sorry?"

"The other day, on the phone—it was really unprofessional of me to say what I did, I mean about your looks. I'm sure it, whatever, like, already sucks enough to be a woman in your line of work, and how people treat you, and I just didn't want you to think that I don't take you seriously as a journalist. I read you all the time. So, I'm sorry."

"Okay. I accept your apology."

"I think you're great."

"Okay."

"As far as the guys who shot up my house, the guys who did this to my face, that's part of the price of doing business. I like to keep a low profile."

"Non-Aligned—is that in reference to the Da Silvas and the Underground Riders? That you're freelancing?"

"Do you know Jawarharlal Nehru? Colonel Nasser? Josip Broz Tito?"

"Yes. Are we doing a twentieth-century world leaders quiz? Do you know, I don't know ... Maurice Bishop?"

Scott smiled. "The New Jewel Movement? Grenada."

Angelique couldn't suppress her surprised laugh. "Jesus, that's impressive. What kind of gangster are you?"

Scott nodded his head.

"My mom told me about him. Look, whatever you've gotta write, I understand you have to write it. Even if it's about Polis. Off the record, here, we're not trying to take anything, *anything*, from the UR or the Da Silvas. Non-Aligned means no bosses, but it's also supposed to mean no enemies. Maybe my house will be hit again. I'm not afraid. Although I get that it was probably scary for my neighbours."

Scott turned his attention away from Angelique, watched a group of kids rolling down the side of a small hill. With every passing minute, Angelique was more confused about who Scott Clark was and what was going on. Who was the Non-Aligned Movement, and why hadn't she heard of them before? And if they were really trying to strike out on their own, would this cute, bruised, chubby young white kid live out the year?

But she hadn't specified that it was Polis that had been hit, had she?

"Do you have everything you need?" he asked.

"I never do," she said. "Here's my card, okay? You want to go on or off the record, reach out."

Scott nodded, looking at the card for a second before pocketing it, giving a low wave, and wandering off away from the waterfront, toward the parking lot. Angelique watched him climb into a waiting car with an Asian guy at the wheel, who drove off as soon as Scott put on his seatbelt.

She turned back to look out at the water and the mountains, wondering if she had time to make it to Car-Free Day. The mystery of Scott Clark and the Non-Aligned Movement wasn't about to come into focus this afternoon.

"I know where I know you from!" said the sunburned dad from behind her now, Logan on his shoulders and Olivia's hand in his own. "You're the crime lady, from TV!"

Angelique nodded solemnly, aware that the crime lady from TV would be spending the rest of her Sunday at the computer.

11

It was a strange thing to hold such a great deal of money between his fingers, and ultimately Scott couldn't help himself from shuffling through the bills, child-like, just to feel the weight of it all in his hand. Five thousand dollars wasn't that large a sum, in the scheme of things, but it was still by far the most cash that he had ever had his hands on all at once, and to begin with, anyway, it was impressive, even if after a while the cash lost part of its magic—the bills were like a word repeated until it made no sense, until it seemed almost hilariously arbitrary and contingent that any group of people would have arrived at such-and-such a term to indicate such-and-such a thing, or that a human society had ever seen fit to draw an equal sign between these little strips of paper-like coloured polymer on the one hand and, on the other, given quantities of everything and anything. Just like it could suddenly become crazy, after rolling the word around in your mouth enough times, to think that there could be a room in your house called a *den*—that you could sit in a *den*, that you could have a fight in a *den*, lose your virginity in the *den;* that English-speaking people had decided that a room in which you neither slept nor tended to entertain company, a room which allowed you to raise the price of a downtown condominium by twenty percent simply by expanding the square footage of a lightless storage space and applying the label, would henceforth be a *den*—it could just as abruptly seem completely unreal to think that an illustration of the Queen, with maybe some birds on the flipside or a portrait of a long-dead prime minister thinking serious thoughts about how to win World War II or keep Chinese people out of the country forever, could be traded for any good or service, legal or illegal, that you could think of: a muffin, a handjob, an artificial Christmas tree, diabetes medication, heroin.

"I read this book a little while ago," said Josiah. "Kind of popular science, but also history. The guy explains how, basically, the whole reason why our kind of human— "

"Cro-Magnon?"

"Homo sapiens."

"Isn't that the same?

"I'm not sure; I always mix that up. Anyway, the point is, he was saying that the reason that we evolved and, like, lasted out over all the other types of humans, Neanderthals and whatever—that basically it came down to our cognitive ability to make stuff up. To agree on fictions and, essentially, shared, made-up values. He said with chimpanzees, it's just brute force, how they organize themselves, but we can have societies because we can all agree to pretend that things are a certain way."

"Except that I'm about to hand over this stack of imaginary money to a Neanderthal, or else he's going to smash my head in with a rock."

"Anyway, that's what he said." Josiah indicated the room, the house around them. "But it makes me think how—it's wild, you know? We're sitting inside over a million dollars right now. The money on the table would barely pay for one of the sconces in the hallway, and yet that biker is going to come in here, take the cash, and leave the rest of it standing."

"Do I have sconces?"

"Don't you?"

"I thought sconces was when a light was fixed to the side of a wall. All the lights in my hallways are in the ceilings."

"I thought 'sconce' was the name for, like, the molding that runs along where the wall meets the ceiling?"

"No. That's just called molding."

Josiah furrowed his brow, then released it. "Anyway, it's all crazy."

"Or, like, you think about a burglar—some guy breaks into a house, and the house is worth a million and a half dollars. And while he's inside it, it's his, I mean, effectively. He commands it. Million and a half bucks. But he can't move it around, he can't sell it. He's gotta content himself to grab a TV, maybe some jewels, whatever, worth not even the beginnings of a percentage of what he's leaving behind."

"Like a bank robber having to throw away the rubber bands around a stack of bills, only the bands are worth a thousand times what the bills are."

Scott smiled, then frowned. "Should these be in rubber bands, you think?"

Josiah cocked his head, giving an indifferent pout. "I don't think it's necessary. Probably an envelope, though—that seems to be pretty consistent in all the shows. Do you have an envelope?"

"I have no idea. Can you check the junk drawer?"

Josiah stirred his hand around the drawer before producing a squarish, card-shaped envelope wreathed in illustrated Christmas holly. Scott winced.

"That looks kind of effeminate, I hand it to him in that, doesn't it?"

"It's not ideal." Josiah looked back down. "There *is* a rubber band in here."

"Let's just do that."

Josiah watched as Scott arranged the bills carefully into a stack, then struggled to fit them with the thick, blue rubber band.

"I think this was from, like, on broccoli."

"Have you thought about how to broach it yet?"

"What do you mean?"

"The Rider. Mike? What you're going to tell him so that he doesn't come back next week?"

Scott raised his palms, then dropped them. He ran his thumb nervously up and down the side of his cheek, then through his hair, then exhaled loudly as he leaned his head back into his hands.

"Did Par ever text you back?" he asked, changing the subject.

"No."

"I'm starting to get worried. I haven't heard from him since right after."

"Do you think ..." Josiah began, before stopping nervously.

"What?"

"Do you think, maybe ... I had never planned to shoot the gun, you know?"

Scott dropped his eyes. "Yeah, I sort of—I thought that was a little weird."

"What? Fuck you!"

"What are you telling me 'fuck you' for? I'm just saying I agree with you!"

"The two of you were laughing like fucking idiots, so I panicked! I'm not a hardened criminal, Scott—I've never done a goddamn hold-up before. Twice now I've shot a gun in the past week, and both times it was to save your dumb white ass!"

"Jesus, Joe, just calm down, all right? You're the one who brought it up, okay? I was just saying, that, like, yeah—it was a little weird or whatever. Or just, I don't know. Unexpected."

"Do you think it traumatized him?"

"No. No, I'm sure ..."

"I didn't mean to scare him. I just wish he would call."

Josiah paced the length of the kitchen, and Scott followed his movements in anxious empathy until finally he texted Pardeep again.

par, j's starting 2 panic bad. U ok? plz shoot a quick message

Almost immediately, he regretted having said "shoot," just as the rumbling of Mike's Harley-Davidson shook through the nearly million and a half dollars of the house.

"Damn it. It's him. What do I tell him?"

"Scott, it's time to wrap this shit up. Enough now. Just tell him the truth."

"How, though? It's too complicated. It sounds too stupid when I say it out loud. He's not going to buy it."

"What other option do you have, though, Scotty? You just gotta try to tell him, and hope he does."

"And if Angelique runs something about me, the hold-up, the Non-Aligned Movement? What happens then?"

Josiah raised his shoulders helplessly.

"Don't borrow trouble, Scotty. Cross that bridge when we get to it. She hasn't run anything yet—from here, it looks like you somehow stumbled upon a reporter who wants a few supporting facts before running a story."

"She's a special lady."

Josiah twisted his face in mild confusion at the turn in the conversation, as Scott nodded solemnly, then stood while trying to decide if he should have the money with him when he answered the door, or whether that was overdoing his submission. He watched through the window as Mike lifted himself off the bike, removing the small helmet that fit his skull like a swimming cap before rolling his arms and shoulders in the same thick-knotted display of musculature that Scott and Michelle had always joked about. Scott's phone dinged.

Pardeep had texted: *Scott we are fucked.*

Mike pounded on the door.

"It's Pardeep. He says we're fucked. What does that mean?"

"I don't know. I think you should answer the door, though."

"But what does 'Scott we are fucked' mean?"

Mike pounded again.

Par what do you mean. r u okay?

"Scott, please—answer the door."

"Do I bring the money with me?"

The pounding sped up.

"Just open the fucking door!"

Scott's phone pinged again: *I'm coming over.*

Scott stared at the screen, then started for the door.

Mike was seething behind a pair of horn-rimmed tortoise-shell sunglasses when Scott greeted him. He smiled with a kind of battery acid sarcasm for a moment, before pushing his way into the house, his hand gripping Scott's throat, slamming his back into the wall.

"I knock *once* next time," he said, pointing with the index finger of his free hand, then slapping Scott, then pointing again. "One time, every time."

"Hey," said Josiah gently, drawing Mike's slightly stunned attention away in the manner of the world's calmest rodeo clown. "Let's all, just—relax, okay?"

"Who the fuck is this?" Mike demanded of Scott, jerking his head toward the end of the hall, where Josiah stood with his palms open, trying to calm Mike as though he were a ghost or a bear. "You trying to ambush me, you little bitch?"

"Look," said Josiah, "there's no reason for anybody to get worked up here, okay? We're just—"

Josiah choked just from the shock of it. The side of Scott's forearm had crashed into the crook of Mike's arm, knocking the hand away from his throat, but the terror made it feel like it had landed on Josiah's. Just as he became convinced that he must have imagined it—that Scott's thrashing back, physically, at this walking, talking sports utility vehicle in an Ed Hardy shirt had to have been a hallucination—he watched dumbfounded as his friend launched forward from the wall and shoved the Rider with the brute force of a chimpanzee trying to convince everyone in the room to share the fiction that he could fight back.

It was impossible to read Mike's eyes through the shades, but Josiah could see that he cocked his fist before releasing it, possibly because of the head count he'd done in the split second since the shove, or possibly because Scott had somehow established a baseline respectability with his assertion of dignity in miniature.

"Little spark, huh? Some balls? You get cute like that again I'm going to put you in the dirt, boy."

The adrenaline was very nearly crackling out of the tips of Scott's fingers, but he kept his breathing even, his posture and his gaze straight, and nodded slightly, submissively; even he could tell that Mike was calming down.

"That's my associate, okay? That's my buddy." Scott drew a deep breath, looking at Josiah, then back at Mike. "This is who shot up my house."

Mike took off his sunglasses.

"Lovers' quarrel?"

Scott tried to calibrate his response; if he accepted the homophobic jibe, did it show that he was chill? Or did it show him rolling over? Mike had seemed to respond well to the pushback, but would he take any further such displays as kindly? Or more likely, was he simultaneously easing the tension while reminding them all who was in charge? While Scott was pondering the sociology of the gay joke, Josiah had been running a different, more productive set of equations.

"Insurance," he answered. Scott could have kissed him.

Judging from the way his face began relaxing, Mike was figuring it all out just a few seconds behind Scott.

"That's what I was trying to explain to you the other day, Mike. I swear to God, we're not running girls, or cards, or drugs, or anything out of here. It wasn't a hit, it was a set-up. It was an insurance scam and it didn't even work. We got in over our heads, that's all. It was a one-time thing."

Scott and Josiah watched as Mike took them both in, took in the house, gnawed his lip in frustration and resignation, reluctantly coming around to the fact that this explanation made more sense than anything else he'd figured on. Scott felt the softness coming into the room and allowed himself to hope.

"I thought you said this was your associate? Are you guys a crew or not?"

Scott shook his head dismissively, buying himself time to think of the most productive answer. "I would barely even call it that. Loose, low shit, Mike. Nothing of any interest up the food chain."

"You know who fucking decides what's of interest on the food chain?"

Scott and Josiah shook their heads.

"Fucking lions, bro."

Scott nodded ingratiatingly "Listen, if this is a UR block—"

"It is."

"No, that's what I mean. This is a UR block. You guys are still owed a taste. The frigging scam didn't score us anything, but as a show of good faith, I have the money you asked for." Mike arched his eyebrow appreciatively. "Joe, grab the stack."

Josiah nodded, disappearing for a moment before returning with the five thousand dollars folded like a soft taco in the thick blue band, which Mike ripped apart with his finger before counting through the bills. He looked up at the two of them.

"This is good. This means at least you didn't waste my time."

"You don't need to come back next week," ventured Scott. The adrenaline was flagging now, his voice catching. As the tense energy shook out of his body, he was afraid that he would cry. "There would be nothing to collect on."

Mike sized the two men up a final time as Josiah nodded. It looked to Scott as though he were trying to suppress a smile before sliding his shades back onto his head.

"You two girls ever go into business again, you put some away for the tax man. I mean anything at all, I'm collecting on it."

They nodded.

"You know Espresso Calabria on Hastings? You can find me there a lot of evenings, or else you can ask to see me. You tell me if there's anything I need to collect on. Or I can pop in here, sniff around. You'll prefer to come to me."

Scott and Josiah nodded quickly, trying not to giggle or bawl just from relief, trying to signal that they were not nothing at all, but also not worthy of anyone's attention—that they weren't mere citizens, but that they weren't big enough fish to get a skillet out for.

They watched as Mike climbed back onto the motorcycle, gingerly walking it backwards out of the driveway before gunning it to life and tearing through the cul-de-sac. Now Scott didn't bother to keep from crying. Now he was safe.

The Dhaliwals sat silently hunched over the blond pine table that Manjot's father had built himself in the late 1960s, working in the tradition of the family's relationship with West Coast wood. Like most of the earlier Punjabi settlers in the area, Pardeep's great-great-grandfather had worked in the sawmills, churning the swathe of the British Empire closest to sunset into piles of furniture, paper, timber. Coquitlam was proudly home to a neighbourhood called Mallairdville, the first Francophone settlement in the area—but the pride didn't extend to its reason for being there, namely as a sop to turn-of-the-last-century racists. When a suburban mill employing Sikh lumbermen was targeted with angry demands to replace their tanned workforce with a pastier proletariat of European ancestry, the owners fired their Sikhs and sought out a group of employees pale enough to appease xenophobes but benighted enough to pay poorly. Luckily, His Majesty's realm contained subject peoples in all hues, and Vancouver's first French-Canadian settlement was born.

The fact that the family had never left the Coquitlam area was a mark of almost unfathomable social stasis; that they had never gathered the necessary capital to pick up stakes and move further west, into the greater desirability of the city, ever closer to the ocean, nor had they ever been broken down to the point of being pushed east, the invariable direction of Lower Mainland failure, was almost impossible to explain. But the rangy area pulling up from the Fraser on one side, the Burrard Inlet on the other, as though for some reason squeamish of water, had been home to the Dhaliwal family on a scale of time that was unimaginable for nearly anyone in the area besides the people from whom it had been stolen.

Pardeep searched his father's face now for the sarcasm or the defiance, the coolness that defined him, but he was just grey, his cheeks and jaw pocked with black stubble, resting on splayed fingers bearing the weight of his head and neck. Manjot was staring at Gurdeep uncannily; intimately, but with very close to nothing in her eyes: no reproach, no solidarity, no anger, no understanding. She had known, too. They'd both told him, but somehow it was clear that it came back to Gurdeep.

"Dad?"

Gurdeep swivelled his cradled chin in his palm, lifting watery eyes up at his son, and raised his shoulders.

"This is life, *beyta*. This is how it works."

When Pardeep arrived, the front door was still open, and the last bottle of rakia that Bojana Clark had ever purchased had been two-thirds emptied into two of the young men she had left behind. Pardeep ran his hands over his ashen face; he was one day unshaven, which put him just past where Scott would have been at three days unshaven, and Josiah at a week and a half.

"Boys?" he said.

Scott whooped from the sofa where he was lying with his feet up, his cheeks the colour of tart plums.

"Pardeep!"

"*Mera bhara!*" yelled Josiah.

"We're in here, bro!"

Although Scott had never asked him to, Pardeep pulled his shoes off as he did every time, for Bojana, pulling the heels down with his toes and kicking his runners into the alcove next to the front door. He closed it behind him and locked it, and made his way into the living room where the Renoir print, a clean line breaking its way down the length of the glass, had been leaned precariously back up against the wall atop the fireplace mantle.

"Buddy," Scott said, smiling, standing to envelop his friend in his arms. "We did it. He's gone. We did it."

Josiah nodded, uncharacteristically optimistic, pumping his fist as he once again refilled his small glass with the sweet brandy that would be kicking in the sides of his head like an unplacated biker the next morning.

"Yup," he added.

"Par, it's rakia time, brother. Grab a drink. And you thought we were fucked!"

"Scott, we are," said Pardeep.

"Is this about getting your parents their money back? It's my number-one priority, Par, I promise. I'll sell the Jetta."

"Probably want to replace the rear window first, gangsta," said Josiah, and Scott laughed.

"Bro, that's part of NAM history! That'd be like sewing Dillinger's suit back together."

"You don't owe my parents anything, Scott."

"No, now, stop it," Scott said, sobering slightly. "I'm not hearing that, man; we are paying them back. I can send the first two grand back home with you tonight, in fact."

Josiah nodded.

"No, Scott. You're not listening to me. You don't owe my parents anything because you didn't take their money."

"I don't get what you're trying to say. Whose money did I take?"

"The Da Silva Brothers.'"

This time it was Josiah who threw up; a perfect pouch of amber, slightly foaming fruit brandy dropped soundlessly from his mouth down the front of his shirt, and Scott dropped onto the couch, unable to trust his knees.

"I don't understand."

"Neither did I," Pardeep said, pouring himself a shot of the drink in Scott's glass. He swallowed quickly, screwing his face up against the burning sweetness, then poured another. Then Pardeep began to cry. Scott rubbed his back while Josiah, now very nearly entirely sober, took off his shirt.

"I've never seen my dad like this," Pardeep continued. "Ashamed, like. Scared."

"But, Par, why?"

"That shit with the cards? The conspiracy theories about Visa and Mastercard? All of it was bullshit. He doesn't believe in conspiracies."

"So he does think Bin Laden did 9/11?" asked Josiah, with the tiny sliver of his mind that was still drunk. Pardeep shook his head.

"I just mean the credit cards. It had nothing to do with that thieves in the night shit. He stayed cash only because he's been washing money for the Da Silvas for years." Pardeep looked to his friends, reading their faces for judgment and, seeing none, carried on. "The way he laid it out, it was all so simple and straightforward. He said nobody at the tax office knows how many cans of chickpeas a Greek restaurant needs for a week's worth of hummus. Maybe it's ten large cans, maybe it's fifty. He said that's how they laid it out to him."

"Who?"

"Nicky and Danny Da Silva."

"Jesus."

"Jesus."

"That's what I said. I don't—" Pardeep started, trailing off and starting again with his voice raised. "I said 'Dad, why? Did you owe them something? Did they threaten you?' And then—I've never seen his face like this, not even when his sister died. It's like he wasn't even sad, he was broken. My mom left the room. He just shook his head. He shrugged at me. He fucking shrugged! My dad. He said they came in one day, asked him was he interested in making an extra few grand a month, without any new risk. No shake down, no threats. Just a business offer that made no sense to pass up. Pass thirty grand a month through the restaurant, keep three of it."

"That's, what—thirty-six grand a year."

"That's about what a receptionist makes."

The brandy evaporated under the force of the solemnity in the room, the three men sitting, breathing, no one saying a word. Josiah stood, moved into the kitchen, and ran his shirt under the water, letting it sit at the bottom of the sink. He rubbed at the tattoo of the baseball on his chest, the tattoo that everyone always mistook for skin cancer, then cleared his throat.

"So, just so I have this all straight—we just stole seven grand from the Da Silva Brothers, and kicked up five grand to the Underground Riders?"

Pardeep nodded. Scott nodded.

"I guess the Non-Aligned Movement just picked sides in the gang war," said Josiah.

"That's not how it's supposed to work," said Scott, and nobody could tell if he was joking.

"Don't be stupid," said Pardeep. "Fidel Castro was in the Non-Aligned Movement. That didn't stop him posing for pictures with Khrushchev."

12

Kevin Dartmouth, who had killed three people several years earlier in Ontario and severely beaten many more in many places since, had suffered from sleep paralysis since childhood. He hadn't known then that it was sleep paralysis. He could only remember what felt like an unbroken string of nights when he had lain awake in his bed, right down the hall from his parents' room, eyes pinned open widely as he was unable to call out to his mother, who should have been able to hear him. As a grown man, he could very clearly remember the suffocating feeling of wanting the words to leave his chest, where they instead stayed leaden and unmoving. What he didn't understand, even in retrospect, was why that should have felt so natural to him; why he hadn't ever thought to mention it the next morning, to either his mother or his stepfather, but he supposed that since that was how things had always been, he had just assumed that it was how things were. It wasn't until he was a teenager and casually, indirectly mentioned it to his family doctor, dropping a line into a conversation about the neck pains he would sometimes wake up with, about "You know, how sometimes when you wake up, you can't move or breathe for the first little bit?" that he was given a name for it, sleep paralysis—the exact opposite of sleepwalking. Where sleepwalkers had a dysfunction in the distribution of the chemicals that keep the rest of us relatively still while sleeping—letting us run through fields in our minds, or take final exams for courses we'd forgotten to drop out of at the beginning of the semester, while actually staying perfectly horizontally in bed—those who suffered sleep paralysis were on the other end of the spectrum, their minds leaving sleep for waking life before the stilling elements had run their full course, rendering them unable to move. Never-convicted murderer Kevin Dartmouth would suffer between twelve and fifteen incidents of sleep paralysis a year, and these had left him with a preternatural fear of suffocation, of the loss of control of his limbs or his body. He had come to believe that Lou Gehrig's disease or multiple sclerosis or even something as simple as a stroke were the very worst things that could possibly happen to a person. He had read the story about that guy who had been in a coma for like twenty, twenty-five years, and everybody had thought he was brain-dead, but in fact, he had been fully conscious and simply unable to move or indicate anything. Kevin thought about that story two or three times a week, and every time he did he had to leave the room, shake his arms and legs, splash his face with water. His belief that to be imprisoned inside one's own body was the very deepest of possible sufferings had been the reason why he, two summers ago, despite not being what anyone would describe as a feminist, had broken the legs and ribs and then neck of an aspiring Underground Riders associate who had laughingly recounted the story of drugging a young woman to the point of motionlessness before violating her. As a full-patch member, the unilateral decision to mete out that kind of discipline had been within his rights, even if some had found it extreme. The young rapist was now in a wheelchair, and would be, moving forward.

None of these thoughts went through Kevin Dartmouth's mind in any salient way as he lay face-down on the floor of the backseat of a car he didn't know, a T-shirt stuffed into his mouth, his hands taped behind his back, the full weight of his friend Patty Baker on top of him. The muted childhood recollections, the terrified mornings after freedom of movement finally made its way to his extremities, the surge of empathy he had felt for the young, drugged woman—he didn't think through any of them distinctly, but rather felt all of them, all at once, on a level that superseded rationality or even memory. He had vibrated his body against Patty's for the first few minutes of the ride, just to know that he could. But finally, he laid perfectly still, waiting—as he had on so many awful mornings—for the ability to move to come back.

Just a half hour before, Kevin and Patty had each been finishing plates of ribs as heavily doused in syrup and cloying sauces as sundaes. All night, they had laughed louder than they'd needed to laugh at each other's stories, called the waitress sweet pea a greater number of times than men three times their age would have, stood as far back as possible from the urinals while pissing, so that anyone who came into the washroom while they occupied it would know where they stood. Patty was a fast-rising associate, and Kevin had a full-patch, and what was it all about if not this? The money to eat and drink; the power to be merry.

It had all felt like a perfect night: a couple of bitch suburban dads being reminded who was boss, a cute little good-sport waitress taking home a forty-percent tip, Kevin laughing suddenly as he waved to Patty with the keys he'd just found despite himself, barely seeing the baseball bat Patty took across the face at what seemed for all the world like the exact second he felt the gun go into his ribs. Then the shirt was in his mouth, and the waking paralysis took hold. Nobody said anything in the car, which was silent for several minutes, until someone put on Phil Collins. Hearing the music, Kevin tried to bring back good memories of his stepfather for comfort. He couldn't. Although he had loved Phil Collins, Barry hadn't been a very good stepfather.

After an impossible number of turns, the car finally stopped, and the warm night air was like a deep-freeze after getting out from under Patty. Kevin stumbled to keep up with his captor as he was pushed and dragged along a short tar driveway and down a shorter set of stairs; all he could see was country—a green darkness, not the grey darkness of the city, and in the small halo of yellow light that shone from the bulb on the side of the house, all he could process was a farmhouse and maybe some woods. In the basement, he was very quickly forced onto a spring cot, watched them handcuffing him to the sides of it as the T-shirt finally came out of his mouth, and he gulped air like a dying man. Patty was set up nine or ten feet away from him, in the same situation.

"Patty, buddy? You with me?" he croaked.

"They fucked me right across the face, bro. I was out for a little bit, I don't know how long."

"Why don't the two of you shut the fuck up?" asked one of the men who was in charge, very calmly and mid-vape, so that his voice was like cotton. There were three kidnappers and the two of them, and they all stood, or lay, in silence for twenty minutes before the basement door opened again, and Kevin got up as far as he could on his side to see who it was.

"Buddy. You like racist jokes, huh?" asked Nicky Da Silva as he crouched down next to Kevin's cot, smelling beautiful, dressed simply but with elegance.

"Fuck you, buddy," Kevin said, his voice sounding like his own again. "I done time with white men and done crime with plenty others when I had to. I don't know what the fuck you're talking about."

Nicky Da Silva's face stayed perfectly still. Then he laid his hand on Kevin's crotch.

"Fuck off!" Kevin thrashed, but Da Silva's men came over to the cot and pinned him. Once again, his movements weren't his own. He began to foam and seethe. Nicky put his hand back, this time as a fist.

"'Long Dong Tam.' That's some very stupid shit," he said.

He raised his fist. He brought it down.

13

The moment that Scott saw Michelle Chong's name flash onto his call display, he regretted having put off phoning Darryl for so long. The conversation with Darryl would have been hard, but now, instead, he would have a conversation with Michelle which would be impossible. And as compulsively easy as it had been to keep sending Darryl's calls to voicemail, one after the other, it was inversely inconceivable that Scott would not pick up a call from the woman who had been his wife.

"Hello?" he said, as a question. People still answered the phone as though they didn't know who was calling, just like they stubbornly referred to phones as "ringing" even though there wasn't a twenty-five-year-old alive who had ever heard them do anything but chime, buzz, or beep. In this instance, Scott felt deeply grateful for the three-second's grace the anachronism bought him. But Michelle had no time for indirectness.

"Scott, what is going on?" she asked immediately before continuing with a kindness and concern that twisted the knife. "Are you okay?"

In some ways, Michelle had been the worst person in the world with whom to mourn his mother, because she had loved her just as much as he did, and Scott knew that the feelings had been reciprocated. From the first time that Scott had brought Michelle home to meet his parents, he had noticed Bojana reacting to her, treating her very differently from the admittedly small sample-size of previous romantic partners to whom she had been introduced. The fact that his mother regarded Michelle so differently made Scott look at her differently, and sped the intimacy of their first months together. After they were married, Scott had never heard Michelle say the words "mother-in-law"; she had always referred to Bojana as "my Mom."

In life, the intimacy had been touching, had smoothed out moments that, in other people's relationships, were fraught. But in death, the symmetry of feeling was crushing. When they found out, together, that Bojana was dead, Michelle had let loose a primeval, moaning wail that the far-flung Serbian aunts and cousins had found jarring, and that Scott found left no room for him to scream. There was no leaning on Michelle because she needed just as badly to lean on him.

Scott had wondered, in retrospect, whether the unmediated quality of Michelle's grief—the fact that it wasn't a reflection of his own, but its own burning source—had made some part of him think of her as a sister, or some part of her think of him as a brother, because in the months after his mother died, what had been a lively and formally experimental sex life became an artifact, a set of memories. The incestuous dampening of their physical lusts had been exacerbated by the fact that he and Michelle had run in different directions from the loss of their mother: for Michelle, it meant that it was time for the two of them to become adults in earnest; to build real, mature, professional and family lives to the extent to which that was possible in Vancouver. Scott had responded differently.

"Hi, Michelle," Scott said now. "Hey, listen—I know this is weird or whatever, but, honestly. Congratulations."

"What? Oh, my God. Thank you, Scott. But can we focus on one thing at a time here? My dad is beside himself. Have you gotten hooked up with some kind of gangsters?"

Scott tried to imagine Michelle pregnant—what kind of pregnant lady she would be. Her sister had been one of the women whose entire body stayed exactly the same, cheekbones like broken dinner plates, with a tiny little mound above the pelvis; but her best friend, Christine, seemed to gain weight even on her nose and lips. Scott could imagine Michelle with that thick, shiny hair they all seemed to get, that luminous skin. She had always had beautiful skin.

"I guess it couldn't be me, huh?"

"What? Scott, what does that mean?"

"I'd have to be 'hooked up' with gangsters? It could never be me who actually was the gangster himself, right?"

"Scott. What the hell are you talking about?"

Scott sighed, turned off by his own peevishness. He had started to make peace with the fact that that aspect of the plan hadn't worked, and maybe that was for the best. Despite his reported non-cooperation with police, no one seemed to think that he was any kind of gangster or that the Non-Aligned Movement was any sort of player in the Lower Mainland scene. Angelique Bryan had failed, so far, to publish anything, even on her blog, about the hardened criminal Scott Clark, about the feisty upstarts of the NAM, and it seemed like all that was probably a good thing—it had gotten him off the hook with Mike, for instance. It meant that there wouldn't be any long-term repercussions.

But there was something nagging at Scott's ego about the impossible time that everyone seemed to have imagining him as a genuine menace. The suburbs were full of middle-class thugs, the muscle-bound sons of general managers and administrators, who nevertheless managed to convince everybody that they were genuine criminals. No one thought of Vancouver's street gangs as collections of sallow urchins anymore, rumbling as much for body heat as out of the economic desperation of a Jacob Riis still. The West Coast had long ago accepted that their new kingpins had grown up going to swimming lessons; that they'd had backyards and, when they didn't have carports, they'd had genuine garages with doors that closed by remote. So why did everyone insist on thinking that *he* was soft, but not them?

"Scott, my dad is apoplectic. He says he's been trying to call you non-stop, but you keep ignoring his messages."

"I'm sorry. I wasn't trying—"

"Do you know what this is like for him?"

"What what's like?"

"Having you turn on him like this."

"I haven't turned on him, Michelle, Jesus."

"That is so unfair."

"How?"

"My father loves you, Scott! Or, at least he did when he thought he knew who you were."

"Michelle, it was all a mistake. I—I think it had to do with the biker who used to live—he owns the house next door. You remember that guy?"

"Muscles?"

"Yeah, the big guy. His name's Mike."

"How do you know his name?"

"I don't know—it doesn't matter. Every white guy that age is a Mike. Anyway, I think he's UR."

"Like an Underground Rider?"

"Yeah."

"Wow."

"And I'm guessing that that's what the shooting at the house was."

"Somebody was gunning for him?"

Scott nodded reluctantly, then remembered that he was on the phone. Here he was, being emasculated by his own criminal fiction, his own set-up. He resigned himself to the fact that, even in a lie, he didn't make a believable target.

"That's why I didn't say anything to the cops, Michelle. I was—" He sighed. "I was scared. I didn't want to tell them about Mike."

"Scott, Jesus—it's perfectly understandable that you were scared. I'm just glad that you're okay."

"Yeah. I'll be fine."

"Listen, I'll talk to my dad, all right? I'll explain it."

"Thanks. Michelle, listen—I spoke with your dad a few days ago about selling the house, but—" Scott swallowed his guilt. "I don't think this would be a good time to do it. With the violence, the shooting, it's going to make the house really hard to sell."

"You mean it might take two hours to get an offer, rather than ten minutes?"

"Right. No, but I'm serious. I know you guys need a place to live, but I just don't think I could take the hit that the loss in value would represent."

"Scott, I don't want you to worry about us right now. We're okay where we are, for the time being. I mean, I would like some space for the baby ..."

"Yeah. So do I. Like, I mean—I want for your baby to have space."

"Right. But I don't want you to have this on your plate. I'll talk to my dad, okay? I'll explain. Don't worry about selling the house."

"Michelle, I—thank you," Scott said. He ran his thumb along his teeth, and he hung up the phone.

14

Angelique missed the presence of other journalists; she missed the days of rooms filled with people writing. But things had become lean; made efficient by becoming worse. Angelique had been on crime for years, spending more time at courthouses and police stations and shot-up coffee houses than she ever did in the offices of the *Star*, but there had nevertheless always been the feeling of a home base; a buzzing, teeming office that, these days, she couldn't remember ever having been irritated by. Now, she could only remember how comforting it had been to be able to talk a hunch through with somebody, ferret out a bullshit source by bouncing their rap off a colleague at the politics desk, the city desk—anyone who knew people and institutions and who therefore knew the corruption and temptation and gullibility and cruelty and kindness that invariably followed in their wake like rats following agricultural settlements or waterworks.

There was something about Scott Clark that didn't add up, but at a certain point Angelique Bryan would have to concede that she had everything she needed to include him as one of the local players, if a minor one (and maybe, given the story she'd just seen on the wire, something more). Her instincts strongly compelled her to slot the ConcernedCitizen12 emails as bullshit—except that everything else, besides her own unscientific sense of the man, pointed to the fact that they weren't. His house had been shot up, and that generally wasn't something that happened to innocent people; someone had given him a serious beating, but he hadn't seemed shaken by it, and certainly didn't seem to be pursuing it legally; he himself had admitted to the existence of his gang, of his founding role in it, and had petulantly hinted, in fact all but admitted, that they'd been behind the stick-up at Polis. Still, she wished she had someone—someone with her seniority, someone who had ten seconds to spare where they weren't doing what used to count as four separate and indispensable newspaper jobs—to talk it over with. Something still didn't feel right.

But now this wire story.

Angelique still had the yearbook from Dr. Charles Best Secondary, Grad 2005, that the school's librarian had reluctantly handed over when she'd asked to borrow it to check against the tip. And there it had been, plain as day. Was she losing it? Or was Scott Clark a bigger deal than she'd been able to sniff out? And why did she find herself personally disappointed that he might not be a decent guy?

LONDON POLICE NAB "THE CANADIAN" AT CENTRE OF DRUG AND COUNTERFEIT SUIT RING

LONDON—Police at New Scotland Yard have arrested Adnan abd-Husseini, 31, the man whom they believe to be the elusive figure known until now only as "The Canadian" among law enforcement officials. Mr abd-Husseini, son of Better Suited men's fashion retailer CEO Farid abd-Husseini, is accused of being the distribution point in the United Kingdom not only for counterfeit Italian suits made in China, but also for vast amounts of heroin allegedly smuggled inside the suits themselves.

"We will be pursuing a massive and multi-layered criminal conspiracy case with Mr abd-Husseini as the end point," said Superintendent Liam Devon. "This marks an illicit international effort tying the maritime powers of organized crime from the triads in Hong Kong through the Camorra of Naples to the very sordid and malicious groups polluting our own British shores with their endeavours."

It is alleged that Mr abd-Husseini used his father's network of men's wear warehouses and even storefronts to receive counterfeit Hugo Boss, Armani, and other Italian suits produced and sold by merchants with links to powerful Hong Kong triads. The suits did pass through the port of Naples, which had for a time worked to obscure their point of origin. It is also alleged that, in Naples, each shipment was augmented with genuine Italian suits, which had been lined with heroin.

Devon explained to reporters that a "shadow figure" known as "The Canadian" has long dogged Scotland Yard's best detectives, and it is believed that Mr abd-Husseini's Egyptian heritage is part of what kept him from being suspected as "The Canadian" for so long.

"To a certain extent the joke was on us, I suppose, and well done," conceded Superintendent Devon.

The nickname likely derives from the fact that Mr abd-Husseini spent his formative years in Canada, first in Waterloo, Ontario, and then in Coquitlam. He graduated from Dr. Charles Best Secondary School in 2005, where, in his yearbook graduation caption, he cited an affiliation to the "Non-Aligned Movement (NAM)" along with report-ed NAM gang founder Scott Clark, whose Coquitlam home was re-cently targeted in a shooting. Mr Clark is not cooperating with police. The Non-Aligned Movement is also rumoured to have played a role in the armed robbery of a local Greek eatery, Polis, though no charges have been laid.

—Global News Service Wire, with notes from Angelique Bryan

15

"He always wanted to watch *Scarface*, you remember that? It was always *Scarface* or *New Jack City* or *The Godfather, Goodfellas, Carlito's Way*."

"So what?" said Scott.

"So it makes sense now, in retrospect," said Par with confidence.

"Get out of here. That is so fucking dumb."

"What do you mean, fuck off? You remember! Whenever we were watching a movie—or, like, any time it was just one of us and Adnan, he always wanted to watch *Scarface*."

"We were fifteen-year-old boys, dude. Everybody always wanted to watch *Scarface*. You're unnecessarily gilding the lily here."

"What do you mean?"

"Speaking of unnecessary—that's redundant," said Joe.

"What is?"

"'Unnecessarily gilding the lily.'"

"But what do you mean by it?"

"Why is it redundant?"

"Because the whole essence of 'gilding the lily' is that there's no need! It's already redundant."

"But how am I even gilding the lily?"

"Because you're trying, retrospectively, to make it all make some kind of sense. Or like he was training up or something. It's stupid. We were young, dumb boys—of course we were into gangster shit."

"It was different with Adnan. He was angry, dude."

"Get the fuck out of here, angry."

"He was, man, I'm telling you. Maybe he didn't trust you with it—"

"What's that supposed to mean?"

"Because you wouldn't know what it's like!"

"Oh, that's bullshit. That's bullshit."

"You remember when he snapped on that kid Nick Bonvino?"

"Kept calling him 'Andy.'"

"Exactly. Man, I'm telling you—there was a streak in Adnan, a core."

"I don't buy it, man. You're inventing a more interesting story. What do you make of this psychobabble, Joe?"

"I agree with Par that there were signs—"

"See? Gilding the fucking lily. Blow me."

"But it wasn't that he wanted to watch gangster movies all the time."

"So then what was it?"

"What Adnan wanted more than anything was cash."

"That's true."

"It's always the Zack Morris types; they're the ones who go in for whatever will get them there. Even in elementary school—I remember Adnan's dad had a Costco membership, and he'd buy those big tubs of sour keys, gummy shit. He had it worked out to where he rode the exact line, like to the pennies, of undercutting Formosa Market across from the school, but still making a profit. Like, they sold their big sour keys for twenty-five cents, he'd sell them for twenty, twenty-two."

"So what? That's just smart."

"Yeah, I mean—I'm no junior capitalist, but that's just hustle, no?"

"You don't think that's messed up? I'm talking he was ten, eleven years old. What kind of ten-year-old fantasizes about turning a thirteen-dollar tub of sour keys into fifteen dollars? I mean, wouldn't you just want to eat it?"

Pardeep and Scott shrugged their shoulders in a soft concession and pulled at the sand-coloured nachos under their sweaty layer of bright orange cheese.

"This place fucking sucks," said Scott. The others nodded.

Each of them had wanted to discuss the seismic news of their lost NAM comrade, the social media phantom and drugs-plus-copyright-infringement kingpin of the United Kingdom, Adnan abd-Husseini, but none of them had felt comfortable going to Polis to do it over hummus or moussaka. Each had avoided confronting their unease directly; there was a collective sense that if they were to speak their reticence aloud, that would amount to an admission that the place had been lost to them, of their own idiotic volition, and that would be too much like losing a home; there was also the matter, now that Scott had been named in the newspaper, of avoiding baffled, heartbroken questions from his friend's parents. Instead, Pardeep had somehow floated the idea of visiting a more properly suburban compound with chicken wings and big-screen TVs running sports-talk panel shows on mute; a place where the waitresses were each attractive in precisely the same inoffensive way and at which the steamed edamame were for some unguessable reason sprinkled with chilli powder.

"You guys want anything else?" asked their young server politely and pertly, and it was a minor concern to each of the three men that they were now at least old enough to find her mildly unsettling.

"I think we're good, probably just the bill please, if you could," said Josiah. The server nodded.

"Sure—do you want these packed up?"

"Old nachos?" asked Par.

She nodded again, this time with less confidence. "Some people take them home."

"Yeah," said Scott. "I'll take them home."

The server nodded in modest triumph, redeemed, and took the plate back to the kitchen.

"That feels like the right move for me now. That feels like where I'm at in my life. Reheating nachos. Maybe not even reheating."

"Just—just don't eat them for breakfast, okay?" said Josiah, and the sincerity of it made Scott flush.

"So, now that Adnan's gangster number one," Pardeep began, picking at his straw with his thumb, "I guess he sort of took you with him, huh?"

Scott gave a joyless laugh, disgusted.

"For that whole first few days, I couldn't get her to run the story. All those emails from ConcernedCitizen12. Then we finally get the gorilla back in his cage and she outs me."

"Do you think this changes things with Mike?"

"Who knows?"

"Well, plus—the Da Silvas now," said Pardeep, dropping his eyes, as he seemed to every time the subject turned to the brothers or Polis or his parents. "She basically said we did the stick-up at Polis on her blog."

"Well, we did."

"It wasn't just her blog," Scott said. "It was in the print edition too. I feel, like—I don't know. I feel like my neighbours are looking at me differently now."

"But that's what you wanted," said Josiah, his voice with just enough flint to betray his resentment at having been pulled into it all. "You wanted them to think you were a big gangster so that no one would buy the house. Well, you did it."

"We did it," said Pardeep.

"Yeah, fine. You both did it."

"Neither of us fired a shot into the bar at Polis for no goddamn reason, Joe."

Josiah seethed for a second, looking at the two of them, then away, seeming to run several scenarios through his head at once. "Fuck you both," he said, standing abruptly and storming away from the table.

"Who wants second-chance nachos?" asked the server of those remaining, smilingly replacing the chips in the middle of the table, this time encased in a shell of Styrofoam.

Pardeep and Scott walked out into the evening where a light, warm rain was falling on the parking lot. The rain was young enough that the mossy smell of summer dampness still hung in the air around it.

"Can you give me a ride home?" Scott asked Pardeep.

"When are you getting the window fixed?"

"Look, I just need a ride home for tonight. If it's a big deal, I can take the bus."

"No, I mean—that's not what I meant. I was just curious."

The two friends rode in a resigned and uncomfortable silence through the relatively quiet, humid streets, Pardeep characteristically waiting until the last possible moment to turn on his windshield wipers and, though he'd been doing it that way since they'd learned to drive, tonight it drove Scott to nearly violent levels of frustration. He watched as the windshield filled with translucent spots growing increasingly Impressionistic until the scene looked like a nineteenth-century French interpretation of the roadscape with oils. Scott chewed the inside of his cheeks, but he thanked Pardeep when they got to his house.

Walking across the damp grass of the yard, Scott stopped beside his mother's hibiscus plant, ragged now but in full bloom, and soon he was kneeling, his legs getting wet beneath his shorts, and then he was crying. He touched the plant, trying desperately to feel that his mother was somehow present in it, forcing himself to the brink of believing in some sort of organic wholeness that could mean that she was, indeed, with him in some material way, by some Buddhist alchemy she would have rolled her eyes at in life but which would allow for her cells to be present in the living, physical plant that he held between his fingers, and as he fell short of believing he cried harder, his shoulders shaking, feeling almost suffocated by the permanence, the immutability and invariability of her not being there. It was such a stupid thought to have, but it was almost impossible to resist it regardless: why did death have to be all the time and forever? In a human world where everything else had gotten less harsh over time, where the punishments meted out had become more humane, why couldn't death be more flexible? Why couldn't there be short breaks?

But it wasn't true anyway that everything had gotten less harsh. It was a spurious premise. His mother—so acidly brilliant, so let down by the indifferent malice of everyone else—would have been the first to tell him that.

He wiped his eyes with the heels of his palms. He raised himself to his feet, left the garden, and headed for the front door which he saw, now, had been busted in.

Both Pardeep and Josiah, his lividness forgotten, were there in minutes; unable to go inside on his own, Scott had sat on the stairs in a rain that fell warm but quickly cooled in the folds of his shirt and the tops of his ankle-socks. When they got there, Scott found his courage, insisting on heading in first, and the men took turns rapidly flicking switches up and lurching into various rooms in the least vulnerable positions they could imagine— fists cocked, or else crouching. The dining room, with its dimmer switch, was an exercise in anxious terror.

Fairly soon it was clear that no one was still in the house. But they had been, and they had been looking for something, because the drawers and shelves had been regurgitated onto the square footage. Scott ran, panicked, to his mother's small jewellery box and found it safe in a drawer that had nevertheless been opened.

"Fuck," said Par, with as much anger as sadness, storming out of the living room and onto the front steps for air. Scott sidled up to where he'd been, next to Josiah.

Scrawled across the now unframed Renoir print, sparkled by the glass that had once kept it safe, then been cracked, and now shattered irreparably, was the crude sentence "DS get PAID."

"The Da Silvas. Danny Da Silva, Nicky Da Silva," said Josiah.

"They want their money," Scott said, then, grabbing a large kitchen knife for safety, though it hadn't been sharpened since Bojana Clark was alive, he headed downstairs to the elliptical trainer, grunting as he lifted the base.

It was still there: the two thousand dollars of Da Silva money that he hadn't paid to Mike. That he hadn't spent. That he had no notion at all of how to handle.

What would Adnan do?

16

In her decades of work, across the half-dozen beats they'd had her on at various papers, it had only happened one other time, but it was a nauseous, unmistakable feeling: when, only after seeing it in print, reading it like somebody else would, Angelique could tell that she had gotten it wrong. Not because she'd jumped the gun, not because she had done anything incorrectly, not because she had projected past what she'd been able to confirm—but because the reality had been considerably more slippery than its constituent facts.

The first time, which had taken angry years to get past—years full of self-disappointment and recrimination, cascading doubts and obsessive, compensatory over-checking on everything else that followed—had been when she was working for a local paper on Vancouver Island and a beloved, multi-term, small-town mayor had resigned from office after a successful battle with prostate cancer had, he told media, shifted his perspectives, his values, and left him thirsty for time at home, with his family. Nothing about the official story had made sense to Angelique, then a young reporter and even more stubbornly inclined to trust her instincts, to equate cynicism with wisdom, and she'd pored over every angle of the resignation, followed up with every possible player, anyone who might have had a different light on things, anyone who could make sense of why a man who'd won municipal elections with near-totalitarian margins, a man who wasn't young but wasn't really that old yet, who could still realistically be bandied around as a possible premier or federal cabinet member, would step away from the game. But again and again, that's what everyone told her. The mayor had encouraged his family physician to speak freely with the press; his wife had spoken lovingly of her support for her husband's decision; his long-time opponents gave gruff, you-gotta-give-him-this/you-gotta-give-him-that interviews saluting his public service. There was a contradiction between what Angelique knew and what she *felt* she knew, but at a certain point, the job dictates treating an instinct just like any other bit of irrational noise surrounding a story. Her profile on His Worship ran in the paper, and only when the newprint was staining her hands did she know with absolute certainty that it was wrong. Two days later, the mayor's purple-faced mugshot, taken on a Hawaiian island where he'd been swerving down humid streets with the blood alcohol level of a disinfectant wipe while on holiday with a local news anchor, emerged online.

What did Angelique know about Scott Clark? What didn't she?

A drive-by shooting—from a U-Haul truck, according to the neighbours. A stick-up at a Greek restaurant, owned by a Punjabi family, the Dhaliwals. A gang that had been extant since these youngish men had been in high school, but which no one had heard or talked about until now, when one of them had graduated to a massive, international criminal conspiracy overseas. What had gone on at that high school?

Angelique poured herself a glass of kombucha from a half-finished bottle in the fridge. She sniffed to see if it was still good, but if kombucha stank to begin with, what would it smell like if it had gone off? Natalie, the only friend she still had from high school herself, had insisted that she start drinking it, with its probiotic goodness, to counteract the course of antibiotics she'd been given to rid herself of strep throat last year. "I don't understand," Angelique had said sincerely. "Are 'biotics' a good thing or a bad thing?" as Natalie had rolled her eyes and refused to answer—and kombucha had since mysteriously become a habit that she couldn't really account for. She took the glass over to her home work desk, where somehow the *Vancouver Star* had stolen even a piece of the place she paid rent to call her own, and began flipping, again, through the pages of the Dr. Charles Best 2005 yearbook.

Scott Clark hadn't been a popular kid, otherwise he would have been peppered more liberally throughout the yearbook. There were pretty girls, pimply athletes, and student council suck-up types whom Angelique seemed to come across again every four or five pages, but besides his graduation photo, Angelique couldn't see Scott Clark. She tried the back of the book for an index, and sure enough, there he was—cited on page 28 (his grad photo) and page 231, just before the index itself, among advertisements from local small businesses congratulating the class of 2005, assuring them of the brightness of their futures, and begging them not to drink and drive. Angelique turned to page 231.

Polis Authentic Hellenic Restaurant
Congratulates the Graduates of 2005
FOLLOW YOUR DREAMS—MAKE BURQUITLAM PROUD!

The ad was written in pointed, ersatz-Athenian font, with columns framing the square. The writing was white text on black, and set in the middle was a black and white photo of the dining area at Polis with four multi-ethnic boys raising their glasses and smiling broadly. Angelique's heart nearly stopped as she read the caption under the image:

"Holding Court": Friends 4ever Adnan abd-Husseini, Josiah
Kim, Scott Clark & future Polis owner Pardeep Dhaliwal

Barely able to breathe or to hear her own thoughts over the pulse in her ears, Angelique turned back to the graduation pictures and read the caption under Pardeep Dhaliwal's: "14/1/13 Zindabad!" She furrowed her brow, flipping to Josiah Kim: "14-1-13 4 Life."

Almost knocking over her kombucha, Angelique shot her hand forward to count through the alphabet. Fourteen, one, thirteen: N, A, M.

The so-called Non-Aligned Movement seemed to count, among its members, the son of the owners of the restaurant they'd held up. Gnawing the nail of her pinky finger, Angelique thought hard enough to squeeze coal into diamonds for a few minutes, then began calling U-Haul locations.

"Ma'am, we don't give out that kind of information."

"Right, I understand. In that case, is there a media liaison who could speak on the record to the *Vancouver Star* about the use of U-Haul property in a violent gun crime? Or would that be you as well?"

A truck, rented from the North Vancouver location on the day of the shooting, by Josiah Kim. Returned the next day.

Angelique laughed and pounded her fist against the newspaper, against the story she had written over the anguished protestations of her best instincts. Adnan abd-Husseini probably had nothing to do with anything; the only real deal in the group and he was flung as far back as the White Cliffs of Dover. She slapped the issue and smiled, tried to think of someone she could call to celebrate her brilliance with, the journalist's nose that she had honed, but the time and energy it had taken to hone that nose meant that no friends leapt immediately to mind. She walked to the sink and poured out her kombucha. She filled another glass halfway with Canada Dry, then topped it with a dark rum. She raised it to the ghost of a reflection in the kitchen window, overlooking a busy Gastown street.

"Scott Clark, you chubby little cutie pie," she said out loud. "You're no gangster."

17

"Can I please get a grande London Fog?"

"Decaf London Fog! Your name please?"

"Um, Scott."

"Great."

Scott considered taking the decaf. It was 3:27 p.m., right at the cusp of where the early afternoon becomes the late afternoon, and maybe a decaf was just as well. But he'd been so terrified by the visit that the Da Silva crew had paid to his house—he'd spent so many wired and shaky hours refilling the drawers and shelves—that he hadn't fallen asleep until close to five, and so he wanted the drink that he wanted.

"Actually—sorry, that was just a regular London Fog. Like, caffeinated."

"Oh! Sure thing," said the pretty, smiling boy behind the counter.

"Great, thanks. Sorry."

"No need to apologize," he said, smiling even more beautifully. There; as it turned out, there *were* some benefits to being among the top ranks of the Vancouver gang hierarchy.

A minute or two later, after an Asian woman with an Irish accent called his name and gave him his drink, Scott sat down next to the window, looking out onto the parking lot of the smaller, satellite strip mall that was part of the larger galaxy of the Coquitlam Centre Mall. He smiled when he remembered the screaming match that his mother had had with a large, bald man who had taken a parking spot that a smaller, more timid man had clearly been waiting for. Having forgotten, or not caring, that he'd left his sunroof open, the large man had told Bojana to fuck off before sauntering into the shops swinging shoulder muscles that no one else could see. To Scott's horrified delight—he was eleven—Bojana had cracked one of the dozen eggs she'd just purchased into the top of the aggressor's car, winking at Scott and the smaller man.

"Can we talk for a minute?"

Scott couldn't tell if he'd heard Mike first or seen him, since each sense impression had come with such a dizzying rush of panic that he'd lost his focus.

"Are you following me?"

Mike nodded, half apologetically, which caught Scott off guard. "From your place."

"Why?"

"I wanted to show you the respect of not approaching you in your home again."

"I'm worth respecting all of a sudden?"

Mike took his shades down from on top of his hat visor and put them over his eyes, staring out into the sunny parking lot.

"You lied to me."

"What do you mean? About what?" Scott's mind and body had entered a plane that was somehow both numb to panic and beset by it; these encounters with dangerous men never stopped being scary, even if part of him now stood outside of them.

"Listen, I'd like to talk to you."

"So sit down." Scott's assertiveness came from a place of resignation, but he could tell that Mike was reading it as confidence, and that little inside joke with himself had the effect of lending Scott a sort of real, actual assurance.

"We can't do it here. Walk with me?"

"Fuck no. I'm concussed, not stupid. We can talk right here."

Mike raised his glasses back onto his hat in muted frustration.

"Listen, I promise you, I just want to talk. I need to run something by you. But this," he said, indicating the inside of the Starbucks, "isn't any good."

"I'm not getting in a car."

"We could just walk the aisles next door," Mike said, jerking his head in the direction of the Save-On-Foods. Scott thought for a minute, then nodded, then stood. The sunglasses went back down.

As they entered the chill of the supermarket, Mike turned to Scott, indicating his face.

"Listen, about what you just said, the concussion."

"I was exaggerating."

"You doing okay?"

Scott squinted in confusion.

"I'll be fine," he said, taking a slurping sip of his London Fog. Mike looked away as he spoke again.

"Listen, I didn't have to approach it in that way, and I apologize if I went about my business in, like, a fucked-up capacity."

Scott nodded skeptically, surprised. "Fine."

They walked in silence for a few feet down an aisle full of baking supplies.

"That Angelique Bryan, she airs everybody's shit."

"At the *Star*?" Scott said, as much out of a felt need to simply say something as anything else. Mike nodded.

"A few years back, some of the Da Silva guys were looking into taking her out. Checked her address and shit and everything."

"That's fucked up," Scott said defensively. Mike agreed, but for different reasons.

"It's stupid kid shit. Reporters are going to report, the idea is you make sure they don't have anything to fucking print. I mean, I understand why they were pissed, but—"

"I think she's brilliant and beautiful," Scott said, and it took several moments for the conversation to recover. They turned down the first of two frozen-food aisles, the blemishes and razor burn on Mike's neck standing out under the neon.

"That shit in her last post, though," he said. "About your work. To make a thing like that happen, that takes a lot of skill, diplomacy."

Scott didn't say anything; he seemed to squint his entire face as he tried to figure out what Mike could mean. Why would it take diplomacy or skill to stick up a restaurant? As he tried for angles that would unlock the mystery, Scott realized that Mike was talking about Adnan. But Mike had already taken Scott's silent confusion for calculated reticence, and folded.

"Listen, I'm not trying to infringe on any of what you've got going on. I only bring it up to say that I admire it, that I underestimated you. Hong Kong, Naples—is that for real?"

Scott shrugged.

He was disturbed by how much he enjoyed being seen walking with Mike. Mike was an oaf and a low-life; he oozed a fog of shitbag machismo and more than likely racism, atavistic greed, and violence, but the fear he doubtless struck in the other shoppers reflected off Scott like the sun's light bounces off the moon. Without meaning too, Scott had adopted the physical bearing of mob-movie tough guys, the useless nodding, the talking out of the side of one's mouth, scratching his face with the nail of his thumb. It was all sickly thrilling.

"You know, I'm guessing that we're into some shit with the Da Silvas right now. A lot of back and forth."

"Miller and Tam?"

Now it was Mike's turn to shrug. "All this shit has escalated more, and faster, than anybody thinks it should. Right now they're holding two UR. One full-patch."

"Jesus," said Scott, feeling the thrill leave his body.

"Look, over there, Hong Kong—the Da Silvas work with those guys too, bringing shit in. They used to use our guys at the ports, actually."

"Right. Okay?"

"What I'm thinking is, given the Non-Aligned are used to sitting down with everybody, making deals, I'd like you to put a feeler out for us. See if anybody on the other side wants to talk."

"To the cops?" Scott asked, his voice cracking.

"What? No. Why the fuck would we want them to talk to the cops?"

"I don't know. I—sorry."

"To us, man. To us. Find out if any of those pieces of shit is interested in peace. Find out what they want—for us to get our boys back. And if there's any appetite, I want you to facilitate."

Scott offered another stunned silence that seemed like disciplined counsel-keeping.

"We'd make it all worth your time, obviously."

Scott tried to speak, and couldn't. Mike grew more desperate, pulling his shades up one more time.

"Just think about it, okay? Here." He signalled for Scott to take his phone out of his pocket, then touched each of theirs together, AirDropping his contact information. "You think about it, and you call me. We can talk at the coffee shop."

"Starbucks?"

"Fuck no. Calabria."

Mike walked briskly away from Scott, and Scott watched as he picked up a foil-wrapped loaf of pre-made garlic bread, mimed it through the self-checkout and left without paying. Feeling his legs shaking underneath him, Scott put off walking for as long as he could, looking instead at his phone to see if he really and truly did now have the phone number of an Underground Rider, the same Underground Rider who had caved his head into the drywall of his own home. He noticed, instead, a missed call from Angelique Bryan's number, followed by a text message.

Can we please talk? There are a few things I would like to follow up on.

Scott reached for his own sunglasses to put them over his own eyes, but he had left them in the car.

18

People had been living where what had lately been named the Fraser River met the ocean for over ten thousand years, and so it was fairly stupid to refer to Vancouver, as people often did, as *young*. Nevertheless, the SkyTrain was only two years older than Scott, and he'd always found that to be a little pathetic.

On a summer trip to Chicago with his family, Scott had been amazed at the ancient smells of the rocking, lumbering L train, whining under its age, and how much it had seen, with even a cloud of rubbery smoke rising up from underneath one of the cars in the middle of an afternoon ride; Scott hadn't known anyone local to ask if that was normal.

Contrarily, the oldest line of Vancouver's light-rail system dated to the mid-1980s; Tina Turner was already long-since broken up with Ike, making much worse music but leading a much happier life. And that Expo Line, named for the third-tier transportation-themed World's Fair that the city had hosted—and where a young Peter Clark had met Bojana Trojanovic, working in the Yugoslavia Pavilion—had for years stood as the lone, pathetic rump of public rail transit in the metropolitan area. The Millennium Line reared up just a few years after the turn of the century that was its name-sake, followed by extensions with sturdier, less immediately dated names, such as the Canada Line to Richmond, or the Coquitlam–Port Moody train named Evergreen, almost as parody.

Scott rode the Evergreen line now to meet Angelique downtown, on the waterfront. She had offered to come meet him, but momentarily having forgotten that the rear window of the Jetta still looked like Bonnie and Clyde's, Scott had instead offered to come to her. It took three transfers to arrive at the beautiful spot on the water, where two different right-wing provincial governments had each built massive convention centres, separated only by about twenty-five years and maybe six hundred feet.

Scott came up out of the station. The first things he noticed, every time he was here, were the mountains, which were bluer than the green ones surrounding Coquitlam. In both sets of mountains, the trees had been sheared like a bad haircut, with houses climbing higher and higher up the sides of the slopes, but the houses he could see from here might be worth close to double the ones he could see from the suburbs. Then he saw Angelique. He waved weakly, smiling.

Now that she was so sure that he presented no danger, Angelique was free to see the almost-drunken crush written on this boy's face, and for a second she nearly felt guilty about the care she'd taken to get ready. She had never been impervious to the fears of getting older, like anyone else, and she had never been able to stop herself from entertaining universal insecurities about the trajectory upon which she'd built her life so far, panicking that maybe she hadn't gotten the best deal when she'd traded so much for her career, but Angelique had never had her friends' anxieties about beauty. She felt fine, and when dates over the years had confirmed it, she'd never said "Really?" but always just "Thank you," nodding and smiling with terrific ease, because she knew that it was right. And she had known that she left this chubby man-boy from the suburbs feeling tongue-tied, and it was possible that she had allowed that to colour the strategy of her preparations for their meeting, that she had allowed herself to smell so fucking good and to have those long, smooth brown arms uncovered by the bright blue, tight blue shirt that she had at least partially chosen for its potentially disorienting effects, to slow Scott's thinking on his feet.

"Scott. Thank you for meeting me."

"Any time."

"There are a few things I'd like to follow up with you about, okay? Is there any place in particular where you'd be more comfortable speaking?"

"Why don't we walk," he said, indicating the Seawall, packed with tourists and cruise-ship passengers. She nodded her assent, then took out her recorder.

"Can we—I'd prefer to do this off the record until I know what this is about."

"Okay." Maybe Scott Clark was more self-possessed that she'd anticipated. They began walking slowly. Each of them slipped a pair of shades over their eyes. "Why did you rob your friend's restaurant?"

Scott stopped for a second, but not for as long as she'd thought, or hoped, that he would.

"Who says I robbed my friend's restaurant?"

"You more or less confirmed for me that you had been involved in the hold-up at Polis when last we spoke. Is that no longer something you stand by?"

Scott rubbed the bottom half of his face with his hand.

"And Polis belongs to your friend Pardeep's parents, doesn't it? In fact," Angelique was bluffing a bit now, moving out into conjecture based on the body language she was reading off Scott who, behind his sunglasses, was reeling. "Didn't you spend a lot of time there as a teenager?"

Scott smiled now, feeling that if Angelique knew as much as she thought she did, she would know that he still ate there all the time. Or at least had, until last week.

"I don't know any Pardeep."

"Yes, you do," Angelique said, her voice toughening. And now she lifted her shades into her thick, perfumed hair, and thrust her phone into Scott's face, showing him the yearbook advertisement for Polis that he hadn't thought about in years. "This is you and Pardeep and 'The Canadian,' Adnan abd-Husseini, whose notoriety you're dining out on. And the Chinese guy is Josiah Kim, who rented the U-Haul truck from which the shots on your house were fired."

Angelique searched his soft face for the response, for the confirmation of her victory, an acknowledgment of her prowess. But Scott only tightened his jaw, then smiled. If there was anything in his face, it was relief. But there wasn't much of anything.

"He's half Korean," Scott said, then laughed softly through a bitten lip, and though Angelique had thought he was cute since the meeting at Rocky Point Park, she now got an idea, for the first time, of how, under certain circumstances, a woman could come around to having sex with him.

"You're not in a gang. You lied to me."

Scott shook his head, his face instantly serious in a way that Angelique found endearing; she spent so much of her time on this job profiling goons and sociopaths and men whose default-violent perspectives on the world did not exclude her, and his evident consideration of her feelings was, in that broader context, touching.

"We didn't know about Adnan, you're wrong. We weren't trying to dine out on him. We found out about all that from your piece."

"What is going on?"

"We're off the record, right?"

"For the time being, yes."

Scott looked again at the mountains. He couldn't bring himself to look at her. "We staged the shooting at my house in order to drive down the property value."

Angelique laughed.

"We got the idea from you."

She stopped. "Raven Place ..." she said, putting it together.

"The only spot in the Lower Mainland where nobody could sell a house. I'm in a position, right now, where I have to buy out my ex-father-in-law, and it means losing the only house I've ever lived in. A place my parents rented for years before they finally scraped together what they needed to buy it, the last place my mother ever lived. You ever lost someone close, Ms Bryan?"

Angelique raised her shoulders, then nodded.

"We were just trying to buy some time. It was stupid, and it caught the attention of some of the wrong people. One thing led to another. I don't know." Scott stopped to let a string of laughing Scandinavian cruise passengers snake their way between them. "You say I'm not in a gang, I'm not a gangster. I say my house isn't worth a million and a half bucks. But if everybody acts like it is, then that becomes what's real, doesn't it?"

"Are you in any danger right now?"

Scott raised his eyebrows in a way that suggested that he didn't know, and he laughed again, this time insecurely.

"Yeah."

"Can you go to the police?"

"No," he said, shaking his head. "But there's a possible way out of this for me, and maybe you can help me with it."

"Listen, Scott, I have ethical commitments to a certain—"

"Angelique, stop," he said, using her first name for the first time. "I would never ask you to do anything like that. I would have hoped, by now, that you'd realize how much respect I have for you."

She felt a heat in her cheeks and on the back of her neck. "Thank you."

"I'm just looking for some information that I can't, like, ask anybody else for."

She nodded slowly, with skepticism.

"In your opinion, the Underground Rider, Da Silva thing, the beef. Can it be fixed?"

"What have you gotten into, Scott?"

"Just—I need to know. What are they fighting over? Is it over real shit? Are they unmovable?"

"From what I understand," she answered tentatively, weighing the ethical risks of each phrase she spoke, "it had less to do with any real, material conflict and more to do with ... personality. Some ill-conceived sexual adventures, then bad jokes turned violent."

"So everybody acted like idiots, showed their asses—and now everybody's entrenched."

"More or less."

It seemed to Scott that Angelique didn't yet know about the kidnapping.

He wondered whether it or the Tam-Miller killings were insurmountable.

"Somebody who wanted to fix it, to bring peace—they wouldn't necessarily have to put anything on the table or have any power to change things in the real world. They'd just need to be able to provide a space where a bunch of meatheads could tuck their balls in for a few minutes and think like people."

Angelique laughed again, and Scott flushed, rushing to take off his glasses.

"I'm really sorry, that was very crude. I don't know—"

"Boy, please. You know my beat, I've heard a lot worse."

"But do I have it about right?"

She smiled. "You've seen a lot of movies, TV shows, and those guys are always smart. That's not the way it is. These guys are stupid, violent young men who find themselves surrounded by a legal and financial environment where their worst qualities can be rewarded with money and, from all the other wrong people, respect. So that means ... you never know. It's like working with kids and animals. It can always go any way. But theoretically, what you're asking—I would say the answer is yes."

"Even with the shootings."

Angelique tilted her head, considering the question, and once again Scott wanted to kiss her. Her eyes narrowed, and for a split second he felt a pang of guilt, thinking that she could tell what was going through his mind. Then he realized that she was processing his problem.

"There's a fantasy these guys have that they're their own government. That's the conventional wisdom about organized crime—that they enforce the rules for people who are outside the rules of the rest of society. But in my experience, in my opinion, that's a myth. Have you read Hobbes?"

"The war of all against all? No."

She smiled. "But you know about the war of all against all?"

"Wikipedia sponging."

"That's cute. Anyway, my point is that these guys, they step outside the rules, and that's it. There are none. They make the rules up as they go along."

"This is why your columns are so conservative."

"Pardon me?"

"Sorry, no. I just mean—you know, you're quite a lock-'em-up type in your columns, I mean. You have to admit, you're pretty law and order, no?"

"And so that makes me a conservative?"

"Well, sort of? No?"

"I see. Please, I've never understood this. Why do left-wing people have such a soft spot for these gangsters and crooks? For the people in our society who act more like capitalists than anybody else? Do you know anything about criminology, about a school of thought called 'Left Realism'?" Scott shook his head. "Well, I suppose there are limits to sponging then, huh?" She jutted her chin at him and smiled, and Scott smiled, then felt the beginnings of an erection and flushed. He was desperately enjoying the conversation, but realized that he'd been put off track.

"So with these guys—killings, kidnappings, that sort of thing ... can they be moved past? Can it ever be water under the bridge?"

"Sure. Or not. Some of them will view those things as the price of doing business in a volatile market. Sometimes money will exchange hands to smooth things over. Other guys will take those grudges to their graves. Sometimes to very early graves."

Scott nodded, then stared at Angelique for a long time before speaking.

"You mentioned ethics earlier."

"Yes I did. I mention them a lot."

"Ethically, I would imagine, that even if you had a story—that if anybody were in a position where that story coming out at a certain time could result in them getting hurt, that ethically you could sit on that for a little while."

"For a little while, yes—if it meant keeping somebody safe who was otherwise going to get hurt."

"And then, ethically, you could tell the story that you had once the situation was no longer dangerous."

"This is Vancouver, Scott—the situation is always dangerous for somebody. Hell, even if it's just an earthquake."

"I know. They keep saying it's inevitable, but I can't bring myself to worry about it. There's just, I mean—there's nothing you can do about it."

"Sure. There's no preparing for them. We've built a whole city of million-dollar homes on land that everybody seems to think is going to rattle or liquefy at any point. But I was speaking metaphorically, Scott. Referring to more sociological concerns, less geological. We live in a strange place."

"Acts of God. My dad, he's become a very religious man recently. I don't see him all that much, but I think that in with the crazy stuff, there's some good stuff he believes."

"My family is very religious, too."

"Like 'blessed are the peacemakers.' I'd say it's pretty hard to argue with that."

"True. But somebody will always try."

19

Sitting in the driver's seat, Josiah took quick, sidelong looks at Scott, worrying his tongue around his teeth and his teeth around his lips, then finally said what he'd been thinking.

"Listen, when we get there—"

"Yeah?" answered Scott.

"I don't think you should order a London Fog."

They drove down Hastings Street for a few minutes, past the driving range and a high school and a strip of storefronts and restaurants, before speaking again.

"I wasn't going to order a fucking London Fog anyway."

"Fine, fine. I'm sorry. I just—"

"What?"

"Nothing. I just know that it's a drink that you enjoy, and I don't think that, in this context, it would be the best thing for you to order."

"Why, because it's an effeminate drink?"

Josiah shrugged, deflecting the awkward gender politics of the exchange. But Scott pushed forward.

"So, like, somehow a cappuccino is macho? Frothed milk and coffee is for boys, frothed milk with tea is for girls? It's fucking idiotic, Joe."

"It's a scented tea, it's flavoured. It's perfumed."

"It's oil of bergamot!"

"Who's Bergamot?"

"Jesus Christ, it's not a guy, it's an orange."

"Hm," Josiah said, watching the road.

"If you want to get real specific, actually," Scott continued, against Josiah's unstated wishes and over the objections of his body language, "it's a citrus fruit that basically helped the Mafia start in Sicily—shaking down the plantation owners and such."

"Great," answered Josiah with restrained impatience. "Make sure to bring that up with the fellows at Espresso Calabria. That way, when you order a drink designed for undergraduates to sip while they watch Lena Dunham movies, the murderous thugs we're sitting down with will know that you're intimately acquainted with their origin story."

"Calabria's not even in fucking Sicily, asshole!"

"Fuck you, Scott!"

Josiah jerked the car over into the parking lane, killing the ignition and trying, with deep breaths, to calm himself. Scott stared out the passenger window.

"Just say it."

"Say. What."

"Just say that you blame me for all of this."

"Scott, what do you want me to say?"

"I didn't have any choice, Joe—"

"Oh, bullshit. Bullshit, man. Scott, fuck. People, people all over the world, they move around. Some of them have to leave their whole countries, for Christ sake. They pick up, they start again elsewhere. It sucks, fine. At least you'd be getting a payout. Maybe it's time to grow up."

Scott gulped for a response but couldn't find one right away. "You think I'm just being selfish," he finally said.

Seeing the dent that he'd left, Josiah pulled back a bit but still seethed. "Scott, I don't know what to tell you. I didn't sign up for this."

"But you're my friend."

"For the time being, yes."

"Nice. And why are we friends, Josiah? What brought us together?"

"Our families happened to live close to each other."

"That's right. And you say it like that somehow makes it cheaper or something."

"That's not what I meant at all—"

"We're not chess pieces, for Christ's sake. You can't just pick a person up and move them someplace else like the space they were in didn't mean anything, didn't make them. That house, that space—you think I want it for the money? That I want to own it?"

"No."

"I just want to stay, fuck, where my memories are. Where the only people who know me or have ever loved me have ever gathered, ever been. Joe, if I lost that place, I wouldn't have anything anymore, I wouldn't be myself."

"And who are you now, Scott? A criminal? Taking beatings, doing stick-ups? You've turned our friendships into a criminal conspiracy. You've pulled me into something, pulled Par into something—"

"Par came with me, like a friend does."

"Fine, you pulled me into something. You want to hang on to the past because it's who you are, as though the act of clinging itself can't do anything to change you."

"It's my home, Joe."

"And who says it always has to be? Who says you get to have it forever?"

"Christ, now you just sound like one of these right-wing developer assholes. You want me to 'adjust my expectations'? Keep adjusting them down, further and further, more and more reasonable every goddamn inch east, every foot smaller? Till I'm living in some cell in a Japanese honeycomb hotel on some farm in Chilliwack?"

"You've got a lot of balls, Scotty. You're one man, all alone, in eighteen hundred square feet. How is that right?"

"I never asked to be alone," Scott said. "The alone part, I mean—that's the whole thing, Josiah. The being alone is why I need it."

"I'll have a double espresso, please."

Scott carried his drink to the table where Josiah was already sitting and took a sip. "I thought a place like this would have better coffee," Josiah said.

"He's late."

Scott and Josiah watched the front door for signs of Mike, taking in the patchy Italiana of the café, its framed soccer shirts and sun-bleached regional flags. Hastings Street began life in the heart of Vancouver's downtown as a stretch of almost impossible urbanity, but the further east it traveled, it shed the city for a lawn-care banality against which Espresso Calabria was almost invisible. Scott sipped at a tiny cup of black coffee for whose benefit it was no longer clear he was drinking, since Mike still hadn't shown up, and none of the old men in the café seemed to be paying them any mind at all.

"Scott," Mike said, looming behind both of them, having emerged from a back door.

"You're late," Scott said, and Josiah almost fainted when he did. Mike looked at his watch.

"It's five minutes, not even, buddy."

"You want to talk here, or should we walk?"

"We should walk."

"Then let me finish my coffee," Scott said, wincing through the rest of the acrid shot as he stood. Josiah stood too, rolling his shoulders in a mimetic approximation of Mike's constant loosening and tightening of his muscles. The three men left through the back entrance, passing a pale group of elders playing cards and speaking to each other in Italian, then out into the lane.

"I've thought about what you asked me," Scott started.

"Okay. Good."

"There's a lot of moving pieces. They've got your guys, but they lost two of theirs, you know?"

"You tell me who says any of that was ever cleared with—"

"Don't," Scott said with an assurance that left Josiah with vertigo. "Don't waste my time or yours. These are the facts on the ground. And I'm not going to waste the Da Silvas' time with a bunch of denialist bullshit, either. They are going to want a tax for hitting Tam and Miller before you get your boys back, and they've got it coming. That's my opinion. And if you're asking me to mediate, that's what I'm going to propose."

Josiah studied both of their faces, trying to sort out whether either of them, Mike or Scott, believed that his oldest friend was a gangster. They both seemed to buy it.

"How much?" Mike asked with angry resignation.

"We'll—we'll sort that out," Scott answered, his eyes betraying their first lack of confidence, and Josiah realized that Scott had no sense of the value of either two lives taken or two released from captivity.

"One hundred grand," Josiah interjected, waiting for either of the other men to blanch. Did he guess right? He watched Mike work through the number and decided to press the advantage. "Plus a finder's fee."

"Fuck that."

"No, that's non-negotiable," Scott said, emboldened by Josiah's intervention and coming to his defence. "That's our fee for putting this together. Fifteen percent."

"Take it, or sort your own shit out with the Da Silvas. The rest of us will be happy to pick up the pieces."

Mike stared at Scott and Josiah, then stared down at the ground and took several long, irritated breaths in through his nose, though neither of them could detect his breathing them back out. He nodded, and they shook hands.

On wobbling legs, Scott and Josiah made their way back through Espresso Calabria, out onto the street, and fell giggling into Josiah's car.

20

"They called us East Indians, and my father always used to say, 'East of what, goddamn it? East of Boundary Road?' They called us East Indians because the others were called 'Red' Indians. The bastard *angreji* needed two different names, one for the people they stole the land from, the other for the people who worked it. You know 'Coquitlam'? It's not even a word. They fucked it from the locals."

"Kwikwetlem. It's Stó:lō."

"See? Scotty knows. And Vancouver, that's just English fucking up Dutch. Van something."

"Wait, does that mean 'Burquitlam' means something, too?"

"No, Par."

"Jesus Christ almighty, who gave me a son this stupid? Robs his own fucking restaurant, and now Burquitlam."

"It's just Burnaby and Coquitlam put together."

"Their travesty of Kwikwetlem, plus Robert Burnaby, another goddamn robber baron *angreji* thief. That's what I'm saying. It's all stolen."

The three men sat morally neutralized in the empty dining room of Polis, each having confessed to their sins, each having cancelled out the others'. Scott and Pardeep had robbed the restaurant, visited minor physical destruction upon it, but Gurdeep had been using it to wash dirty money, and now he was running down a list of the crimes of the British Empire as a way of putting their mutual larceny into perspective.

Pardeep had never seen his father so confused as when they'd told him about the robbery, looking for a second as though he were going to rip the table from the wall, then just as quickly resigning, as though he were blaming himself. "But why didn't you just come to me, ask me, *beyta*?"

Pardeep had shaken his head, doing everything he could to keep from melting, collapsing.

"We should have, Mr Dhaliwal," Scott had interjected. "Everything was ... clouded."

"And now? It's clear?"

"Soon."

Gurdeep had been reluctant to call his contact in the Da Silva organization until Scott had shown him the tightly-packed envelope with the two thousand remaining dollars and promised to hand it back with contrition. Now they were waiting for Gaspar Ferreira, a Portuguese enforcer who had grown up on the Azores where he had worked as a plough horse until moving to Vancouver in his teens and becoming a nightmare. Gaspar had done his first time in prison as a fifteen-year-old, after pulling an East Vancouver vice-principal renowned for his toughness out of his car and slamming him repeatedly into the side of it over what Gaspar had taken to be uncharitable language directed at a friend during an assembly.

Scott tried to make eye contact with Pardeep across the table, and when he did, he indicated around himself with his eyebrows and smiled. Pardeep had no idea what he meant. Scott laughed and dismissed the exchange with a shake of his head. But since having levelled with Gurdeep about the robbery, Polis felt like home again.

"That's him," said Gurdeep, staring out at the parking lot as a white Camry turned its lights into the windows before killing them, along with the engine.

Gaspar turned sideways as he came through the door of the restaurant, and as he did he gave the impression that it was the only angle at which he'd fit. Ferreira was the kind of man who it was impossible to fathom had once gestated inside of another person, as though a quail's egg could hatch a mastiff. He moved through life with the confidence of a man who could never be strangled, since no one pair of hands could ever wrap themselves around that neck.

"Yeah, Gurdeep," Gaspar said with just a hint left of a bouncing Portuguese accent. "You've got something for me?

"Gaspar, yes. Please," Gurdeep said, and Scott felt guilty about surprising him with the change of plans.

"Actually, no."

"What?" Gurdeep and Gaspar had asked the question at the same time, in two different registers, spanning menace and panic.

"Scotty, Gaspar is the fellow I mentioned to you. He works for—"

"I know, Mr Dhaliwal. I know who he is. And I'm sorry, Gaspar, but I don't have anything for you. I've got money for Nicky and Danny, that's all. And something I need to talk to them about. You take me to them."

Gaspar turned his empty eyes to Gurdeep in cretaceous confusion, then turned angrily back to Scott.

"Give me the fucking envelope, faggot, or I'll stuff your boyfriend's dick in your mouth."

"Gaspar, please!" said Gurdeep.

"If he was my boyfriend, wouldn't I *want* his dick in my mouth?" asked Scott petulantly, and Pardeep laughed, then clapped his hand over his mouth.

"I meant I'd rip it off, bitch!"

Pardeep recognized nothing in his friend's response. Scott's face, his words; they were someone else's completely, delivered with absolute assurance: "Listen, I'm looking at you, I can tell math isn't your strong suit. But there's three of us, one of you. So fucking try me, sweetheart. The internet loves mourning dead gorillas."

"What the fuck is this, Gurdeep?"

"I don't know, Gaspar. It's nothing we can't deal with. Let's all try to calm down, right?"

Gaspar lunged at the three men as Scott pushed the table forward, Gaspar falling over it in a blind, animal rage. He grabbed at Scott, who leaned back onto a neighbouring table, tipping it over after grabbing a fork and managing by a lucky shot to stab it into his assailant's ample cheek. Gaspar Ferreira grabbed the side of his face and fell back onto the floor. Scott knew that he was more shocked than hurt, and so he spoke quickly.

"Listen, there's two thousand dollars in here," he said, hoisting the envelope. "I've got an offer to make to Danny and Nicky face-to-face that's going to make them one hundred grand. You leave here with this envelope, you don't bring me to them, I got no choice but to tell them you lost them ninety-eight thousand dollars."

Gaspar was rubbing his red cheek now with the back of his hand, breathing deeply and glaring acidly at Scott.

"Actually, it would be a hundred thousand dollars he'd lost," Pardeep said, from where he was standing next to his father, now holding a serrated bread knife. "I mean, they're still getting the two grand with the sit-down. So all in all, the visit with you is worth one hundred and two thousand dollars."

"Fine, up to you. Makes no fucking difference to me who puts the pill in you," Gaspar said, wheezing. "I'm parked outside." Scott smiled.

"No, I'll follow you, please."

Gaspar pulled himself up to standing, stared at the Dhaliwals with a face like he had carpet cleaner in his mouth, then wedged his way once more through the door.

"Pardeep," Scott said. "Can I borrow your keys?"

"What in the fucking hell was that, Scott?" asked Gurdeep.

"I'm sorry."

"He could have killed us, *bhenchode!* What were you thinking, you stupid asshole?"

"I knew you wouldn't let me do it if I told you. But this is the way it's got to be. I'm fixing this, Mr Dhaliwal, I promise. I'm sorry. I'm so sorry. But I've got work I still need to do. Plus, you know. A reputation now."

Gurdeep stared at Scott, then Pardeep, then raised his hands and dropped them in dismissive disgust. "I'm surrounded by goddamn imbeciles and half-wits."

"Wait, what did *I* do?" said Pardeep.

"Everything is going to be all right," said Scott.

"Oh, well," Gurdeep said. "When you put it like that, fine."

21

Pit bull owners, more than any other dog people, want strangers to love and lavish compliments on their animals. It helped, in this case, that the pearly grey dogs that Scott had read about in Angelique's column were just as gorgeous, smooth, and sinewy as any he'd ever seen. It was immediately clear, once Scott released the first volley of kind words, that only Nicky Da Silva had any affection for the animals—that for Danny, they were merely biological weapons, an alarm system, and very evidently nothing more. But Nicky was full of facts, explaining how loving the dogs were, full of rhyming slogans about banning deeds and not breeds, promising that his girls wouldn't hurt a fly. Then, with a perceptible degree of irritation, his older brother brought the subject matter to a close, reasserting the animals' primary purpose.

"Those bitches wouldn't hurt a fly, but I've seen them pull a man's calf muscle off without jerking their shoulders." The description was vivid enough that Scott was left with the distinct impression that this was anecdote and not abstraction.

There are few things in life more cruelly unjust or capricious than families made up of one beautiful sibling and one ugly one, but that's what God had done to Danny and Nicky Da Silva. It was the kind of thing that ought to be a reproach of vanity or superficiality, pointing up the unfairness of beauty, its state of completely unearned advantage—the same family features played out on two different faces, first as beauty, then as farce; it was deeply unfair, and Scott could tell instantly that Nicky Da Silva had done everything he could to develop enthusiasms and talents that would compensate for the grotesque burlesque he presented of his brother's countenance.

Danny, his dark eyes bright, no smile but still holding a bit of warmth on his face, asked Scott to sit down. Scott had planned to do everything he could not to be too visibly impressed by the house, and it was easier than he'd thought it would be. There were a few large, gaudy pieces of furniture, but for the most part it was empty floor and wall space, besides a portrait of Pope John Paul II hanging beside a large silver crucifix. What was impressive about the Da Silva home was how completely relaxed, even extravagant, they were with square footage that three-quarters of the city would have killed for.

"Before we start," Danny said, indicating Gaspar, to whom Scott now turned in his seat, nodding apologetically until Gaspar bashed the side of his head with an elbow made of concrete. Scott's limp body fell onto the edge of the coffee table, overturning it and emptying several glasses of water and a bowl of *chevda* onto himself and the floor. Gaspar then kicked him in the ribs in a way that made Scott realize that, if they were ever stranded together on a desert island, Gaspar could, and likely would, eat Mike the Biker.

"Okay," said Danny, stilling Gaspar with his hand. "Sit back up and tell me what you came to say."

Scott fought down the urge to puke, squinting hard against the stars he saw in front of his eyes, just like in the old, usually-racist cartoons, and lifted himself back onto his seat. He looked up at Gaspar, locked eyes, and nodded. Gaspar nodded back. Danny Da Silva smiled, and Nicky Da Silva replaced the bowl of *chevda*.

"First of all," Scott said, reaching into his pocket.

"Simmer," Danny said, though they had searched Scott on the way in.

"No, the envelope," Scott said, producing the two thousand dollars from the pocket of his cargo shorts. He lifted it, turned to Gaspar, and Danny nodded his muscle over to fetch the package. Danny looked inside the envelope for less than a second, then raised his shaking head.

"It's light, gotta be by five, at least."

"Yeah," Scott said, catching his breath. "That's about right. There's about two grand in there."

"You stole seven grand though, right?"

"Yes."

"Right, so ..." Danny waved another of Gaspar's punches down on Scott, this time right in the chest, and he was certain that his heart had burst.

"Where's the rest of the money?" added Nicky uselessly.

"Listen—and listen, just keep your fucking goon at heel for two fucking seconds, all right?"

"Watch it," Danny said quietly. Scott doubted that he had ever yelled.

"We did not know whose money this was. I apologize. I'm returning what is left, with apologies."

"But where," Danny asked slowly, "is the rest of it?"

"It's gone," Scott said, just as slowly. "And again, you have my apologies. But with your permission, I'd like to write that mistake off, in light of a much bigger transaction I can help you to effect. One hundred grand."

"Fucking faggot—where's our money?" growled Nicky, but Danny shook his head.

"Let's just sort this out first. What's this one hundred grand transaction?"

"The two UR soldiers you kidnapped—"

"Shut the fuck up."

"What?"

"I don't know what the fuck you're talking about," Danny said, standing, and Scott held up his hands in supplication.

"Look, I—" Scott tried, but Danny ripped open his shirt. "Oh, Jesus. Jesus Christ, it's not like that. I'm not—"

Danny lowered his face to meet Scott's eyes, and Scott realized that this was as scared as he had ever been. All of it, every flight-or-fight response he'd ever had, every anxious tic of biology, had been leading up to this. Feeling rushed in from his fingers and toes, leaving his limbs in order to collect with an unbearable energy in the middle of his chest.

"You did not kidnap anyone. I know that now to be true."

"I have never kidnapped anyone."

"I know."

"You know that?"

"I do, yes." Scott tried to think, but his mind wouldn't move. His mouth went first. "Two men were kidnapped recently, though. Two men associated with the Underground Riders. And they would like your help to get them back."

Danny stood for a few more seconds, humidly breathing a light smell of Crown Royal into Scott's face before smiling gently and taking a seat. "That's different."

Scott nodded his agreement and gratitude. "It is, yeah," he said, and Nicky Da Silva laughed. "I've been authorized to put together a meeting where you and the UR can iron out your differences on neutral territory. I will guarantee everyone's safety. You guys can air whatever grievances need airing—"

"My friends are dead, son," Danny said with an impossible frigidity. "Tread fucking easy."

"And their friends are missing," Scott said soberly and waited for a balled fist or reproach, but none came. "The last few years have been good for everyone. No one wants another full-fledged war. Nobody wants the cops keeping them out of restaurants downtown, nobody wants to spend money on an arms race that's no good for anybody but a couple American cowboy gun-runners. It's time to bring all this shit to a close."

Danny Da Silva didn't say anything, which meant that Nicky and Gaspar stayed in silent contemplation too. Scott continued.

"I've had my beef with the UR in the past too," Scott said, stretching the truth to breaking, but wary of outright lies. "But I can say with some authority that there are people on the other side of this who know that what happened to your friends was wrong—"

"It was a fucking travesty."

"It was. It was a travesty, and they know that. And they're offering to pay a tax here, put some money down that keeps their friends breathing and goes some small way, some very small way—"

Danny shook his head. "Infinitesimal."

"An infinitesimal way toward making things right by your friends' families. And they forget that their boys went missing for a little while, went camping."

"And I forget your five thousand dollars."

"And I forget that you sent men to my house, into my home, rooting through my dead mother's things like fucking hogs at truffles. We all forget a great many violations and indignities, with the greatest offenders making a show of apology in the only way that's left to do so. And then we all move on with the business of making it in this impossible town."

Danny stood from his seat abruptly and left the room, heading into the kitchen. Scott could hear the tap running and Danny filling a glass of water. From a room on the far side of the kitchen, he heard someone stirring awake on a couch, asking in a soft, high, broken voice what sounded like a disoriented question in a language that Scott didn't understand. Danny answered sweetly in the same tongue.

He walked back into the room and stared at Scott, taking long sips from his water.

"Okay," he said. "Set it up."

22

"You know, it's funny, looking back. Your mother and I had such a fight when you were a baby about whether or not we'd baptize you. I was very cynical about it—my mother and father were such proud Anglicans, I wanted to do it just to keep them happy. They already thought your mother was a communist, and I figured, 'What the heck, it's just a few drops of water.' But your mom was so adamant, and she had just carried you, so my vote certainly counted for less. And that's probably as it should be, isn't it? And I remember, she said—because your birth was very hard, I don't know if she ever told you that? You were resting your chin on the ball of your fist and that made it harder to deliver you. You didn't want to leave! And your mother, she said to me, 'During that whole time, in pain and in terror, I wasn't calling out for God, I was calling for the doctor. I was calling out for drugs.' But Bojana was right, you know? For the wrong reasons, but that's how God works sometimes. In her wisdom, even from the wrong sightlines, she allowed you to have the chance to meet Christ on your own terms, to choose, as an adult, when and how to join the brotherhood of Communion."

"Yeah, that's a riot," Scott said.

Scott regretted his sarcasm, but it didn't seem to matter—the beaming widower full of Christlove that was his father had moved into a place of peace and guilelessness that was beyond irony. He couldn't hear the sarcasm; like a fundamentalist can't see his child's evident homosexuality because he won't even entertain its possibility.

It was still not entirely clear to Scott exactly which denomination his father had joined; it seemed, from the outside, to be like one of the Amish or Mennonite-type ones, but to begin with, Scott was cloudy on the difference between Amish and Mennonites, except that Mennonites seemed to him to be slightly more chilled out; they were the Anglicans to the Amish Catholics in the Anabaptist world. Scott had mistakenly labelled his father a newly-minted Lutheran at one point, and had set himself up to be on the receiving end of a long lecture about Luther's perfidy, his greed, his betrayal of the German peasantry and their godly fury. Luther had sided with the landlords, when even a child could tell that the Kingdom of Heaven would never be built by those who owned property. His father's sect seemed to be for those who had come to Christ later in life, the religious equivalent of a high-end online dating service catering to boomers who didn't trust the internet. When Scott passed the hand-painted but professional-looking YOUNG BRETHREN IN CHRIST sign on the highway in a rural area, he would wonder how "young" corresponded to the largely middle-aged group of prayerful farmers, but that was his only real consternation. The Young Brethren Church that his father had joined, in what was either the fog or the clarity of grief, seemed to be at the more or less lucid end of spiritual and the harmless end of kooky.

Peter Clark emptied the Mason jar of cold, mildly sweetened lemonade into his gullet and smiled at his son. "It's nice, isn't it?" he asked, indicating the fields. Scott smiled and nodded. It *was* nice—in the city, everyone's grass had been brown and brittle for weeks now, the few short and feeble bouts of rain during the summer having been insufficient to call off the water advisory, but the fields here were deep browns and greens, rich earthy colours redolent of months earlier, when it seemed like the melted snowpack from last year's mild winter might be enough. Big blue plastic barrels scattered around the heart of the property, outside of the gender-segregated dormitories, the dining hall, and a small wooden chapel, had been gathering rainwater all year long, insurance against dry days such as these.

"Dad, I'm in trouble. And I need your help."

Peter's face fell. "What is it, Scotty?"

"I need a space for some men, some ... dangerous men who are not my friends but who need to meet with each other."

"Yes?"

"They need—I need to provide them with a space where none of them will feel threatened or ambushed. They need a place where they can speak freely to each other, where they know that no one is watching or listening to them."

"Right. Scott—"

"Hold on. I don't want for there to be any miscommunication here. I need you to have a full picture of what is going on. I don't want to make any trouble for you or for the Brethren—"

"The Young Brethren."

"Okay, sure."

"'The Brethren' are a different thing. On the East Coast."

"In any event, having these guys here on your farm could cause trouble for you. But there's also a good chance that it won't, and a lot of good could come out of the meeting if it goes well."

"What kind of good?"

"Very good. An end to recent violence. Two men who are being held captive would be set free. There's a lot at stake. Money, too, so long as we're being honest."

"I see." Peter winced momentarily at the mention of money, then returned to the blank kindness that was his default expression. He reached out and put his hand over Scott's.

"Scott, without judgment, can I ask you—what have you gotten yourself into?"

"Dad, I don't even know how to explain it. It's—it's gang stuff."

"Gang stuff?"

"I made a mistake. I was trying to hold onto the house, and there was no way to do it honestly. I tried something to buy time, and it backfired. I'm trying to fix it now."

"Do you owe someone money?"

"No. I mean, like, yes. I do, but that's not exactly the problem. I owe money in the same way everybody else does. This other problem, this is new."

Peter allowed a second's worth of frustration to pass across his eyes and brow before calming again. "Scotty, you have made a mistake, but it's not the one you think."

"Dad, honestly, look. I don't have time for spiritual riddles. What I need—"

"You equate that house with your mother, and she's not there. Don't get me wrong, she loved that house. Even when we were renting it, she cared for it like it was her own. Her garden—you remember her flowers? She planted a hibiscus tree when you were—you must have been ten, eleven? She loved that house, Scott, but that house wasn't her. It isn't her."

"We look at these things very differently, Dad."

"Make me see."

"I don't think I can. I'm—I'm happy for you, for what you've found here. But that's just it, in a way. I mean, moving forward, it takes having someplace to land. I don't know what's left for me beyond that house. Our home. You travel lightly, Dad, and I respect that about you. I need something to be, to hold onto, or else everything will scatter to the winds."

Peter nodded and smiled and turned and watched the field for a few moments.

"Sometimes—" Scott began. "Sometimes It's like being trapped in a box; I can't breathe. The weight of it, the forever-ness. Two years, Dad. I mean— don't you miss her?"

"Always," Peter said, smiling, turning a wet face toward Scott and tightening his grip on his son's hand. "She was so happy you were gone while she disappeared, Scott, but that's what happened. She was eighty-one pounds when she died. Your mother, who thought that anyone who stopped at one hamburger must have a flu." Scott laughed, doing his best to hold his weeping in his chest. "She was my life and she lost her physical form entirely, and that's when I decided that nothing solid could matter. That every important aspect of our humanity, built with love in God's image, takes place on an immaterial plane."

"And that's fine, Dad. It's beautiful. But I don't know." Scott nodded, an affirmation unrelated to anything that he was thinking or saying. "You left me holding the bag. I don't know any other way to say it. I wasn't ready to let all that go."

Peter nodded. He ran his hard, open hand down the side of his son's soft cheek.

"The dining hall."

"Sorry?"

"For your meeting. The dining hall would work. At nighttime, it's quiet. There are no windows, it's enclosed. Two different doorways, so hostile parties could enter from opposite sides, and neither need feel like they were in the other's space. But I would like to be there."

"No, that won't—"

"You're my son, and I will protect you by whatever meagre means I have to hand. This is a condition. You may not use the space otherwise."

Scott thought for a moment. He stared out at the fields, thought again about how perfect it was, and considered that, even as a grown man, his father's presence brought him comfort and a sense of safety, even if he couldn't exactly say why anymore.

"Okay," he said.

"Scott, no judgment. Have you joined a gang?"

Scott sat silently for a while.

"Scott?"

"I don't know, Dad."

23

"Should we have guns?"

"Well, that's a moot point, isn't it?"

"What do you mean?"

"Because we don't fucking *have* guns."

"Your dad's rifle, though?"

"Jesus, this isn't a chain gang, Par, for Christ's sake. I can't stand there with a rifle like it's goddamn *Cool Hand Luke*."

"No guns," Scott said. "No guns. On them either. You guys search them before they enter the building. We're responsible for their safety. They just need to see each other, exchange the money for the hostages."

"Will I be picking up the hostages too?" asked Pardeep, with a sharp panic entering his voice. "Doesn't that make me an accessory to the kidnapping?"

"I don't—I'm not sure. Joe? You think they'd bring the hostages with them?"

Josiah's eyes widened as he shook his head. "I have no idea what the expectation is."

"Fuck it," Scott said. "Either way, it's not going to be a deal breaker. They each agreed to the terms. We're there to keep things cool."

"We're non-aligned," Pardeep smiled. Josiah shook his head impatiently.

"There's fifteen thousand dollars for us out of this. Five for each of us."

"Listen, Scotty," Pardeep began. "About that—"

"No, that's the split. Three ways. We're a gang, or aren't we?" Pardeep smiled again; Josiah kept a steady gaze. "Guys," said Scott. "There are no words. I just—thank you."

Pardeep nodded and hugged Scott, grabbed his keys, and left to pick up Nicky and Danny at the meeting place in Langley, the 1 2 3 Family Restaurant; Josiah would be picking up Mike and another UR in Maple Ridge, at a donut shop that also sold fried chicken. Neither side could know, in advance, where the summit would be taking place. Scott would drive straight there. It was close to half past eight, and the late August sun was already sinking. Josiah made his way to the door.

"Joe."

"What?" he asked, turning.

"There is more than thank you."

"Yeah?"

"I'm sorry."

Josiah smiled without joy.

"Joe, after tonight, if that's it—if you're walking away from this friendship? I understand. It would kill me, but I would understand. It hasn't been right, and it hasn't been fair. And it hasn't been right or fair in really big ways, ways that I know will be hard to forgive. I'm sure Par would feel the same way if he weren't doling out general amnesty, so as not to get too hung up on what his parents were doing. You didn't ask for any of this. And I—"

"Scott, that's enough. You're rambling. I get it."

"Right."

"I have to go now. I'll see you at your Dad's."

Pardeep's wheels ground into the dry dirt and stones of the path leading to the farm, making rubbery popping sounds as he parked where Scott had told him to, then turned and indicated to the Da Silvas—just the Da Silvas, whom he had patted down on their way into the backseat, and no UR hostages—that although they were parked at this end of the dining hall, which could barely be made out in the country dark, they would be walking to the door on the other side.

"But look, I mean—you can see that we're the first ones here besides Scott. That's his car."

"I don't know what kind of car Scott drives," said Danny Da Silva. "He was in this one when he came to my house."

"Right," Pardeep said. "Right. But that's his car. I promise we're good getting to the hall. I swear on my life—"

"Yes. That's right."

Pardeep swallowed.

"Listen, I mean, we can go through the entrance on this side—"

"Do you have the situation under control, or don't you?"

Pardeep stared at Danny Da Silva in the rearview mirror, then decided that the best course of action was to leave the car and start walking. He didn't see Danny smile after he did so. Pardeep turned on his phone's flashlight and guided the two brothers down the dark, tidy path.

A few minutes later, Josiah pulled up between Pardeep's car and Scott's, with Mike and an older, less muscular, but likely just as heavy Rider named Frenchie in back.

"Everybody else is here," Josiah said, the first words exchanged since Mike and Frenchie had entered the car at the donut shop. "And this is our door. But I need to search you guys before going in."

"Fuck that," said Frenchie, failing to elaborate. Mike, holding a large gym bag and a small backpack, each full of cash, on his lap, held Josiah's gaze in the mirror's reflection.

"Frenchie, buddy," Mike said. "Those are the terms."

"He's not fucking touching me, *hostie*," he said, his jowls barely moving.

"Shouldn't it be a comfort to know that we've searched both sides before anybody went in?" asked Josiah.

"I look like I need comforting from you, slope?"

The silence in the car turned chippy, dangerous. Josiah seethed, and Mike seemed torn between embarrassment and tribal solidarity.

"You fucking assholes asked for this meeting," Josiah said finally. "And that small bag in your friend's hands, that's already ours. You want to be a prick about it, turn the guys who belong to that bigger bag into my best friends, then keep acting like you're scared of airport security. You'll be pretty easy to pick off, waddling back up the highway to the donut shop, you fat white piece of shit."

Frenchie bared his upper teeth at Josiah, then laughed without warmth and exited the car, raising his hands up in surrender, ready to be searched. Josiah waited a few long seconds before carrying out the frisk; he knew that if Frenchie could feel his hands shaking, it all would have been for nothing.

When the last of them entered the room, the Da Silvas stayed sitting, and the Clarks, father and son, stood and nodded.

"Who's this?" asked Mike evenly, pointing at Peter with his free hand, the other lugging the bags.

"That's my father, Peter. This is his place."

Mike nodded, then took in the room, its walls hung with decorative quilts, its carved wooden peace sign, its large wooden cross.

"It takes a little bit of getting used to," said Danny, as Mike, Frenchie, and Josiah sat at their own table, across the room from the Da Silva brothers and their escort, Pardeep. Scott and Peter sat at a third table, at the head of the room, holding court.

"I want to thank you guys for being here. Just being here, that's a start. That's a show of good faith," said Scott. Everyone nodded. "And Mike, I see those bags. That's good. We're here tonight to squash this beef. Some very bad things have grown out of what should have been minor disagreements, handled between adults, between bosses. I'm going to speak frankly here," Scott said, trying to still the catch in his voice, his heart trying to burst its way out of his chest with a broadsword. "Very frankly. There was some Mickey Mouse shit that should have been handled much sooner than it was, and now we're in a place where the bigger problems that came out of that are threatening the professional atmosphere that we're all trying to work in."

"The butterfly effect," Mike said.

"Sure," said Scott.

"How so?" asked Nicky.

"Small things, like a butterfly flaps its wings, it makes an earthquake on the other side of the world."

"How the fuck is that?" asked Nicky.

"I'd prefer," said Danny, "for us to stop speaking in goddamn euphemisms and cryptograms. Our friends Wayson and Brody are dead. That's not small."

"And you've got Kevin and Patty, *maudit sauvages!*" yelled Frenchie. "And I'm still pulling pieces of fucking eight ball out of my ass, *sacrifice.*"

"Let's everybody simmer down, all right?" Scott said, just as Mike's face turned to him in angry confusion.

"Wait," he said, and though Pardeep, Scott, and Josiah each knew what was coming, they still felt the dread knot of anxiety in their stomachs. "Where are Kevin and Patty?"

"They're safe," said Danny without reassurance.

"What the fuck is that supposed to mean?"

"It means what I just said. They're safe. You want them to stay that way, there's a bag you've got for me, no?"

"Sure," Mike said, nodding angrily, and reached for the bag at his feet. "I got a bag for you, motherfucker." Mike stood now, pulling a glock from the side compartment of the gym bag and aiming it at Danny.

"Fuck," said Josiah.

"Mike," said Scott.

"Scott, I had your guarantee," Danny said.

"They're fucking dead, your friends, anything happens to us," said Nicky. "And that's only the beginning."

"Goddamnit, Mike, you asked for this meeting. We had an agreement."

"Then where are my boys? How is this the agreement? I'm going to paste this fucker to the wall."

"It's the worst thing, and the last thing, that you will ever do."

"Motherfucker!"

"Fucking bitch!"

"Each of you boys is wrought in God's image, each of you is born in sin and slavery, and each of you is redeemed in the love and brotherhood of Christ who died for your sins!"

The room fell silent as Peter stood, his hands outstretched, a beatific look on his face. Mike, still holding his gun on Danny, stared at Peter with a face that was desperately trying to figure out what the angles were.

"Dad," Scott said. "Please?"

"Son," said Peter. But he wasn't talking to Scott. He was addressing Mike. "I'm not going to ask you if you believe in God. We men, we people— but let's be honest, mostly we men—we're so ... silly that way, as though our own belief, what we know or don't know, is the central fact of the universe. I don't have to ask you if you believe in God any more than I would ask you if you believed in your own parents' love for you—an echo of God's own love for all of us, his children. I was a father to this boy here, at my side. And I held him with the same all-overcoming love that I know your own mother and father had when they held you. None of us grows enough or hardens enough to take that fatherly love out of God's gaze upon us. The only cost of that eternal love, the only thing He asks us in return for it, his only condition for a love without conditions? Is that we try to show our tiny, imperfect human version of it toward all of his children. This man, sitting across the way from you? He is your brother. Take his life and, like Cain, you are taking the best part of your own."

Mike slowed his breathing.

He took the gun off Danny.

He pointed it at Peter.

"No!" Scott shouted, but Peter pushed him down into his chair.

"Crazy fucking wacko," Mike said. "You setting me up? I'll ice you before anyone else."

"I'm not afraid of your bullets."

"Yeah? Why not? Because you've got a Bible in your breast pocket? How about I put it through your eyes then, instead?"

"That's fine," Peter said, his voice shifting out of the timbre of a sermon and into the tenor of a dad-joke. "I've got the Bible in my head."

There was quiet in the room.

Frenchie laughed, then Danny laughed. Scott swallowed, and Peter smiled.

"Give me the gun, Mike," said Scott. "It's not too late for us to talk."

"Sit the fuck down, Mike, *calice*," said Frenchie. "You asked for the fucking meet. You packed the *hostie* cash in the bags." Mike stayed standing, dropping the gun to his side.

"Here," said Danny, staring at his phone, tapping out a message. "I've got my boys texting a photo of Patty and Kevin, safe and sound and waiting for you at a Starbucks in Whalley." The phone dinged, and Danny passed it to Scott, who slowly took it over to Mike. Josiah and Pardeep exchanged terrified glances, silently begging the other to telegraph a plan. Mike stared at the phone. "After the meeting here, which you asked for, but which you are doing everything in your power to fuck up, if everything goes right from here on in, I send the big bag home with my brother. Scott leaves the small bag here with his father. Your friend goes home with Scott's over there. And you, me, and Mr Clark will drive to that Starbucks together, and you will walk away with your friends."

"And there will be peace upon the land," Peter added.

Scott extended his hand softly, and Mike handed back the phone.

"Okay?" said Scott.

Mike looked down at him, back up at Danny, back over at Peter, and down at Frenchie. Frenchie gave a resigned nod, his face at peace, and Mike gave Scott the gun.

"The saviour said, 'I am the bread of life. Whoever comes to me shall not hunger,'" said Peter. "For the rest of the meeting, let's have snacks."

24

There were no handshakes, but there were no further threats of murder, and Scott was left with the overall impression that, as far these things went, this was more or less how they were supposed to go. The incident with the glock in the bag, which could have been literally fatal to anyone in the room, and figuratively fatal for the ostensible peace talks in which all were engaging, had amazingly precipitated a reciprocal generosity of face-saving excuse-making—Danny had even saluted Mike's evident if inappropriately displayed loyalty to his kidnapped friends, though Scott had the feeling that this magnanimity owed more to Danny's genuine desire to make the deal; that he was excusing himself as much as his opposite number.

There had been a few points raised about sales, about territory and mutually beneficial shipping and wholesaling arrangements, dark corners of unofficial capitalism were cleared of dust and cobwebs, and since Scott had no actual power to grant any concessions he simply adjudicated, solemnly guiding the enemies toward cooperation. Angelique had been right—the problems had mostly been caused by explosive egos and genital taunting, and smooth business operations offered both groups of men an incentive to consign the past to the past.

As the talks ended, everyone stood and gravitated toward their rides. Peter took Scott by the shoulders, and the two men exchanged loving near-smirks at the surreal evening they'd just experienced. Scott collected the small backpack with fifteen thousand dollars and asked his father to hold it for a few hours. The idea of Pardeep riding alone with Nicky and Josiah riding alone with Frenchie had raised in Scott's mind the old riddle about the farmer trying to move a chicken, a fox, and the chicken feed.

"Scott," said Josiah *sotto voce*, tapping him on the shoulder. "I'm sorry. I fucked up."

"How so?"

"The gun. I didn't think to check the bag. I—"

"Josiah," Scott whispered, "you don't owe me any kind of apology. I love you, man. We did it. And each of us has got five grand walking-away money."

"No, Scott. Me and Par—we both want you to have it. Take the money, put it toward the house."

Tears welled in Scott's eyes, and he smiled. "It doesn't matter, Joe. Fifteen thousand. The house will eat that in minutes. It's gone. But we got through this. I'll see you tonight, back at my house, okay? Back at the house."

"But you're not, Scott."

"Not what?"

"You're not through it yet."

"Formalities."

The men walked in the dark to their cars, barely visible in the feeble porch light thrown by the Young Brethren dining hall. There were omnidirectional grunts of goodbye, and Scott, who was still holding the glock, now tucked in the back of his waistband, took the gun and placed it in the trunk of his car.

"Mike, once you're with your boys and Danny has gone, you get the piece back, okay?" Mike nodded. Danny did too.

Everything had been said in the dining hall, or at least everything that could be said, and so Scott turned on the radio as he pulled out onto the Trans-Canada Highway and was surprised to hear the voice of an angry white man complaining about bike lanes and the Canucks' weak defense.

"What happened to oldies?"

"It's sports talk now," Mike said from the backseat.

"Isn't there already a sports station? They really killed the oldies? No more CISL 650?" Mike nodded wistfully in response.

"This city is dying," said Danny, leaning his arm out the passenger window.

Nine minutes later, as they approached the exit for 104 Avenue, Scott saw the red and blue lights splayed like sun rays across his broken rearview mirror, and all the gravity in the world pulled his stomach into his ass.

"Fuck," said Mike, as Danny did too.

After handing over their drivers' licences, all three knew that within just a few seconds, the constable would realize who he had on the line. Mike and Danny read the rearview mirror like a stock-ticker, while Scott sat calmly, putting the pieces together. He looked out through the open window at the sleeping mountains, the cool quiet night of his imperfect home. He spoke with confidence when it was time.

"The gun is mine, but I have conditions."

"That fucking gun."

"What are the conditions?"

Scott turned in his seat, dictating terms.

"Kevin and Patty, they walk right now. They're out. You guys hold to the peace. That's one. Danny, you make the call."

Mike nodded as Danny hunched to text.

"What'd they say?"

"Give it a second."

"Okay, two is Polis. Danny, I want you to ween the Dhaliwals from the laundry service, but I don't want them to feel it too hard. You guys work something out. They get severance, but they're done washing."

"That's up to them, I'm afraid."

"No, it isn't. It's up to me, and those are the conditions for you walking away from this car, and me going to prison."

Danny stared through the windshield while the sound of Mike's breathing filled the car. "That's fine," Danny said.

"Three is that you both send the word, all the way down the line, that nobody fucks with me while I'm gone. My bid, that's going to be it for me, I'm cashing my chips. This is my first and my last time behind bars. The whole time I'm up, I want a Riders honour guard and any stray Da Silva soldiers letting everybody inside know that I'm in there to get fucked by the calendar, and only by the calendar. If that's amenable, then—the glock is mine." Danny nodded.

"Mike?"

"Only if Kevin and Patty walk now."

"That's what I said," answered Scott.

"So then? You heard back from your man yet?" Mike asked Danny.

"No," Danny said, slightly embarrassed by the delay. "But, Jesus, Michael, it's your gun he's saving us from."

"Cops don't know that. It don't have my goddamn name on it."

Scott watched the mirror and saw the constable open his car door, standing behind it, waiting.

"Mike."

"Fuck this."

"Jesus Christ, man, the deal is just as much for you as for me. In fact it costs you nothing. I'm the one who needs to find a new laundry for three-and-a-half hundred K a year. I'm the one with the headache."

"So why aren't your men answering?"

"I don't know, Christ. They have their hands full."

"Bullshit. You never sent the message."

"Tell me why I wouldn't?"

"Because you're a hateful, slippery fuck."

Scott watched the back-up vehicles arriving, the sounds of the sirens slipping in behind the pulsing in his ears. "They're going to ask me to open the trunk, guys."

Mike screamed: "There's no fucking deal until this piece of shit's phone rings!"

They sat in silence.

Danny's phone did not beep or buzz.

Mike's did both.

"It's Kevin," he said.

We're out.

As the RCMP officers, fingers on their pistol grips, approached the car, each bringing an unsteady energy out into the night air with them, Mike shook Scott's hand. Several tears ran down each side of Scott's face, and both of the other men pretended that they hadn't noticed.

Scott picked up his phone and sent a message to Angelique, this time not from a concerned citizen but from an active participant.

Sorry for the short notice, but if you want to come and break the story of The Peace, do your best to make it as quickly as you can to Highway 1, just east of the 104 Ave exit.

Scott looked up from his seat and smiled, seeing a familiar, handsome face with braced teeth.

"Oh *Saint-cibole*," said Constable Gaulin. "Not this fucking guy again."

25

"IT'S ALL OVER!"—3 ALLEGED LOWER MAINLAND GANGSTERS STOPPED, 1 CHARGED

Angelique Bryan

SURREY—RCMP officers from Surrey and Coquitlam believe that on Friday night they may have stumbled onto a "peace summit" after stopping three alleged Vancouver-area rival gang leaders riding together in one car. Scott Clark, 30, co-founder of the Non-Aligned Movement (NAM), was arrested and charged with possession of an illegal firearm. After questioning by police, alleged Da Silva family boss Daniel Da Silva, 41, and full-patch Underground Rider Michael Portland, 36, were released without charges. A rivalry between the two men's organizations is believed to be at the root of a long summer of Lower Mainland gang violence, which began with the brazen mid-day murders of alleged Da Silva associates Wayson Tam and Brody Miller outside of a Kamloops eatery in July.

The car carrying all three men was initially stopped headed west on Highway 1 for a traffic infraction, when a constable behind the vehicle noticed a broken rearview window. The broken glass was the result of a shooting earlier this month at Mr Clark's residence in Coquitlam. Several more cars were called to the scene when the constable realized whom he had stopped.

There were no official statements from RCMP on the significance of having found the three men together. But one officer, speaking on condition of anonymity, was cautiously optimistic.

"It looks good. Ideally, when we see these guys sitting down to talk, it means everybody's tired of the violence. We'll see what happens over the next few weeks, but personally, I think it's a very good, hopeful sign."

It is unclear whether Mr Clark, shouting audibly from the back of the police cruiser in which he was being detained, shared the constable's optimism—though he was visibly smiling as he yelled: "It's over! It's all over!"

When asked why he was carrying an illegal firearm, Mr Clark was equally cryptic, saying, "Because in Coquitlam, we don't play. There's no pretending, baby. NAM till I die!"

Neither Mr Da Silva nor Mr Portland offered any comment.

26

The year Scott spent in prison was easily the worst year of his life, but it had been a pretty easy life, up to that point, and so that offered a bit of context.

Both Mike and Danny had been true to their words, and Scott had gone into his cell having already made all the friends he'd need to stay relatively safe and comfortable. Four months into his bid, just as he'd begun to feel the power of the initial vouchsafe wearing off, a Rider named Kevin Dartmouth, a man with a Mosaic aura that split seas of yard-thugs effortlessly, was sent up for a trafficking charge and brought with him a seemingly boundless reserve of loyalty to Scott that allowed him to spend his time inside reading, working out, and, with some help from Angelique's research, establishing a correspondence with an old friend.

> *Brother, what an amazing thing, to hear from you, after all these years. Looks like we both went rogue. I had a good run—they're so racist over here, being a brown guy called "The Canadian" was as good as being invisible. Once we're both out, you'll have to visit, bring the rest of the NAM boys; you'll meet your NAM niece and nephew, my Fatima and my Saeed, the lights of my life—the reasons for all of my stupid misdeeds as well as for my early retirement. Brother, do keep writing. I miss Vancouver. I even miss Coquitlam.*
> *Adnan*

Now Scott was free, and in his freedom, he admired the kitchen sink, which stood where the elliptical trainer had been; he took the whole thing in and smiled. Almost fifteen-thousand-dollars-on-the-nose worth of renovations. And prison had seen to it that he didn't need an elliptical anymore anyway.

"I can't believe you did this," he said, crying again, this time making no effort to disguise it. Josiah placed his palm on the back of Scott's neck.

"It was never going to work with five grand, Scotty. And it was your scam. We're just—I'm just glad you're home, brother." The two men hugged, and the baby cried upstairs.

"It's not soundproof."

"I wouldn't want it to be soundproof."

"The door at the top of the stairs locks from both sides. The laundry room is shared, but otherwise, that's it. Did you want to go up and see Michelle and Luis? Meet Jimena?"

"Michelle's got her hands full. I'll pop upstairs later."

"She left that," he said, pointing at the hibiscus flower floating in a clear glass bowl filled halfway with water, a card reading WELCOME HOME!!! leaned up against it. Scott smiled warmly, listening to the sound of the baby wailing upstairs.

"Let's go to Polis," he said.

"Under new management," Josiah smiled.

"I have to see this."

The shift in authority that had taken place at Polis while Scott had been away was underwhelming in its effects. Although Pardeep had technically and officially taken the helm, Gurdeep still heckled him back to work when the reunion hug lasted for longer than the marketplace dictated it ought to.

"Okay, okay, it was a year. You're not married!" he said, eyes watering, pushing his boss-son away in order to slap Scott's back himself.

"Buddy," Pardeep said. "Goddamn did we miss you."

"You just saw him, shit! Not three weeks ago!"

"Oh my God, Dad, it's not the same thing! He's out, for fuck's sake."

"Don't swear in my place."

"It's my fucking place."

"Bloody fucking kid," Gurdeep said, batting a hand in surrender, walking back to the kitchen, past the debit sign and the credit card reader. Pardeep smiled at Scott.

"What do you think of my place?"

"It's a truly authentic Hellenic experience."

Pardeep and Josiah smiled.

"I'm going to go get you some hummus."

"No hummus, please. It still tastes like an ass-kicking to me."

"Tzatziki?"

"Please, Par. Thanks."

"Your friend is here."

"Yeah?"

"Over by the window," Pardeep said, indicating with a sideways nod.

"I'll give you a minute," said Josiah.

"I'm going to run out of thank yous here."

Scott approached Angelique's table and made sure that he was watching her eyes as they crawled up his post-prison body.

"Jesus, boy. You lost that baby fat."

Scott smiled as Angelique stood and hugged him, and he could smell the perfumed August sweat on her neck and thought that he could die now. He hadn't seen her since a quarter of the way into his sentence, as she had been completing the last interviews for her second feature to win the National Magazine Award: "The Make-Believe Gangster Who Brought the Peace." Scott had bristled slightly at "make-believe," but staring at her now, that face, that perfume, he was willing to take all slights, all blows.

"Ah, moussaka. A woman after my own heart."

"There you go. You know what? I'd take it over lasagne."

Scott smiled. "So? What's changed since I went away?"

Angelique did an exaggerated parody of thinking deeply, of consideration.

"Well," she started, "the houses on Raven Place are selling for eighty thousand above asking price ..."

"So all is right again with the world."

"Something like that. And ..." she said, flaking the sides of her potatoes with her fork. "I've accepted a buy-out."

"What? You're not serious."

"Unfortunately, yes."

"That's unbelievable. Jesus, Angelique—you just won a National Magazine Award. Your second one!"

She shrugged. "And I wasn't writing about hockey or cars, so fuck it, right? It's like it didn't happen. They said the current climate didn't support crime as a distinct reporting category. That it could be covered along with all the rest of the news."

"No different from the rest of what's going on."

"Maybe they aren't so wrong, sweetie."

Scott blushed.

"What are you going to do now?"

"I'm not sure. It was a decent package, all things considered. I've got at least a book in me, maybe more than that. And there'll be some money for it."

"Will you write a chapter about me?"

"I don't know if there's a whole chapter there ..."

"Ouch."

"What are you going to do?"

"No clue at the moment. If I were smart, I'd monetize my infamy."

"Yeah, that's how the winners do it."

"It's not insane actually, especially if you write your book. We could go on the road, give talks together. We'd be a show they'd pay for, the cocktail-speech circuit, dinners, that kind of shit. Lots of money in it, you find the right agent. Plus, we'd get to hang out. The retired gang leader and the retired crime reporter."

"Retired? Hell, Scotty, there are certain words you do not use when you are trying to flatter a beautiful woman who's reached a certain point in her life."

"Former. Sorry."

"That's only a little bit better."

"What do you think? Would you go on the road with me?"

Angelique smiled. She took a bite of her moussaka.

"It's an idea, I suppose," she said. "Separate hotel rooms, though, right?"

"Of course," Scott said, confidently. "Everyone needs a place to call their own."

ACKNOWLEDGMENTS

As a fourth-generation Vancouverite, I feel deeply rooted and at home in a very beautiful place that I am nevertheless not indigenous to; in a story about the scramble for space in an off-the-wall colonial-settler real-estate market, the first acknowledgment should be to the Squamish, Musqueam, and Tsleil-Waututh nations, on whose unceded traditional territories I live and work.

The characters in this book—each and every one of them—are fictitious. But if there's anything realistic about the world they inhabit, I owe it to the sorts of details unearthed by the brave and diligent journalism done by the *Vancouver Sun*'s Kim Bolan. I also made use of the true crime writing of Jerry Langton in helping me to more fulsomely imagine a fictitious Lower Mainland crime universe. The science book to which Josiah makes reference is *Sapiens: A Brief History of Humankind* by Yuval Noah Harari. The story of bergamot and the origins of the Sicilian mafia can be found in John Dickie's book *Cosa Nostra: A History of the Sicilian Mafia*. Meditations by David Harvey on housing, and by Stan Persky on the arbitrariness of beauty, in their books *Seventeen Contradictions and the End of Capitalism* and *Buddy's*, respectively, were jumping-off points for observations made by the characters and narrator of this novel

My friend Sam Wiebe guided me gently through the process of writing my first crime novel, and I'm deeply grateful for that, and to Naben Ruthnum for putting us in touch; I'd also like to thank CBC's Sheryl MacKay for having asked me an interview question about "guilty pleasure reading" that helped me get the ball rolling on this attempt at joining the genre squad. Thank you to Tejpal Singh Swatch, Alexandra Zabjek, Rob Simmons, Ryan Knighton, Stephen Hui, and Paul Bae for notes, thoughts, and encouragements.

I am deeply honoured, and a little heartbroken, that the manuscript for this book was the last one edited by Susan Safyan in her position as in-house editor at Arsenal Pulp Press; she is smart, funny, sharp-eyed, and makes everybody's books better. Thank you, Susan.

Thanks also to the entire team at Arsenal: Brian, Robert, Oliver, Cynara, and Shirarose; thank you to Zoe Grams of ZG Communications; many thanks as well to my literary agent, John Pearce, at Westwood Creative.

Love and gratitude as always to my family, including my brother and father and their partners; and to my aunts, uncles, and cousins. To my daughter Joséphine, and to my wife Cara—who is doing the hard work of organizing structured, electoral civic resistance to the profit-driven gutting of our beloved city—I can only reiterate how happy I am to get to share this space with you.

My uncle, Phil Birnie—who built the second half of his life in Coquitlam, and who was one of the very smartest and very funniest people I ever knew—died in the summer of 2017, while I was still writing this book, and he didn't get to read much of it. Regardless, it's for him.

CHARLES DEMERS is a comedian and playwright, and the author of several books, including *The Horrors*, *The Dad Dialogues* (with George Bowering), and *Vancouver Special*, a finalist for the Hubert Evans Non-Fiction Prize. He has appeared multiple times at the prestigious Just For Laughs festival, is a regular on CBC's *The Debaters*, and is the voice of Walter the Slug on the Emmy-winning Netflix cartoon *Beat Bugs*. A longtime political activist, Charles lives in East Vancouver with his wife and daughter.